ABANDONED HIGHWAY

a novel

C. WADE NANEY

Grindl Press

ISBN: 978-0-9826216-0-8

GP

By the Same Author

FICTION

The Dews of Night

The Bensford Spring

NONFICTION

Model T Education:

INSTRUCTIONAL

Increase Vocabulary by Reading
Franz Kafka's Metamorphosis

Increase Vocabulary by Reading
The Secret Sharer

Increase Vocabulary by Reading
The Strange Case of Dr. Jekyll and Mr. Hyde

Increase Vocabulary by Reading
Voltaire's Candide

ONE

THE RAINDROP fell warm on the back of my hand — unusual for the time of year. I looked up at the scattered, dark-rimmed little clouds. Not yet big enough to make real rain, they were only playing thunderstorm games. The field of blue they played in was as pure and deep as the waters off Andros Island. I shifted the seabag to my other shoulder.

The guitar case bumped on my buttocks as I trotted across the highway. It and the seabag were all I carried. The bag had been with me for four years; the other, a little longer. Very little that I had owned four years in the past was still mine.

A strong gust of southerly wind rudely welcomed me home, lodging a dust particle in the corner of my eye and blowing my collar up Elvis-style. Behind me, a metal Greyhound sign fluttered like mallard wings, and from several directions, loose tin popped on gins and grain bins. Safely across the highway, I dropped the bag, straightened my collar, and dabbed the particle from my watery eye, surrounded by the smells of tractor grease and school books and prom perfume that were not really there, that lingered until the sounds settled and my vision returned.

Heaving the bag back onto my shoulder, I stood at the intersection of the only highway through town and the only street leading through the business district several blocks away. Mooney's, I could see, was still doing business at the corner, but I didn't recognize the kid pumping gas. Wearing his grease proudly, he squinted at my dark figure between the place he occupied and the late afternoon sun. I nodded. He squint-nodded back. He may have recognized me. I may have recognized him less four years and an acre of hair.

Last year's cotton lint still hung from the highline wires down the road to the Co-op Gin. Crossing the railroad tracks, I headed downtown. The station-house still stood, vacant and boarded, last year's maize stuck in the cracks of the crossties. A greenery smell that I didn't recognize filled the air, but everything else was familiar: streets with no litter, cars parked down the center of Main the two blocks of downtown. Up ahead, I saw that Old Mose was not on the bench in front of Smiley's Hardware. He'd probably died. But Old Somebody Else was there, so it didn't matter.

I passed the open door of the domino parlor. Voices inside were relaxed, joking. From two corners came the sharp slap of domino against card table—in rapid succession from one table. Mexican dominoes. The sharper sound of cue balls came from deeper within. Something new.

Old Somebody Else strained up his head as I passed the hardware store. "Evenin'," he gummed at me. "Evenin'," I returned. I heard him cover my tracks with tobacco juice as I walked on.

My footsteps echoed under the store awnings. The shaded sidewalk was cool, the wind still. For a time I walked unaware of my surroundings, aware only of the great changes in me since last I'd known this street—and of the changes I knew I would soon see in others. *On the other side of the world, a war was dying down. A quarter of a world closer were places I had been.* And not only my remembered actions but all of those places, all of that intervening time had caused those changes in me.

A car full of teenagers lazed by, headed for the south Main Street turnaround. A girl passenger stared moon-faced at me. The car's radio played music sung in protest, music I had not heard on these streets. If the teenagers shared or understood its sentiment, I couldn't tell.

Ahead, I recognized a mongrel, dirty-white with black splotches all over. He'd crossed the street behind the teenager car and was now stopped at the curb, intent on my approach, dripping spit. Maybe he recognized me, as well.

Farrell's Dry Goods was closed. Out of business. Behind the great glass: blackness. A tall, blue-jeaned figure gazed back at me, his hair ruffled from two thousand miles of airline and bus travel. Whatever military bearing he'd until recently assumed was now gone. His seabag looked out of place against the store window. Old memories of denim workclothes and cotton print dresses crowded it for space. The seabag moved on.

I crossed the street. More cars were parked than seemed necessary to conduct downtown business, but I could not see the people who belonged to them. The teenager car went by once more, headed for the north Main Street turnaround. Moonface stared again. Teenagers seemed younger.

From McWhorter's Super Market emerged an old woman followed by a shopping basket pushed by one of the El Bartleys. Elwood, Elvin, Elbert—I couldn't tell which. This one wore the same close-cropped hair style of the others, in spite of the times. With a touch of gray and bib overalls, he would have been his father. They crossed in front of me to the old lady's car. She smiled an old-lady smile. Her eyes twinkled. I smiled back. Mine felt dark. Her big blue Oldsmobile shone like a gemstone. I wondered why small town old men sat on benches in front of Smiley's Hardware and small town old women drove big, shiny-blue Oldsmobiles to the grocery store.

Turning the corner at the pharmacy, I walked into the sun resting behind two long, red clouds hanging low over the horizon. Behind the clouds the sky was white turning to silver, the little clouds now dark blue with silver and gold faces. The whole spectacle reigned over the High Plains like a scene from Cecil B. DeMille. Nowhere else, I thought, but the sea.

Around the corner the sign for the town's last departed doctor was still in the window. On the curb the "Doctor Parking Only" lettering had almost faded away. The First Baptist parking lot was empty, but the ghost of David Brandon sat on the parsonage steps. I kept walking. No sidewalks existed beyond the church grounds. I walked on the edge of the pavement. Down one side street, the high school. I glanced once. Two blocks ahead—home. Home without Daddy. I strained to see if Mother might be in the front yard with the flowers. She wasn't.

Strange—I'd expected everything to appear as though my four years away had been a weekend out of town, but it was as though someone had played chess with the neighborhood. The pieces had been moved around; fences and trees, obviously there for years, I didn't recognize. My footprints should have been on the grass.

For a gnawing moment I felt the absence of the sea. Stepping into the past suddenly became less comfortable than venturing into unknown waters. Like this home place, the sea was always familiar but always changing. But at sea the change was expected and exciting. In the last few years I had witnessed much: storm and calm, oceans blue or green or silver, touristy beaches and filthy harbors. My leave-time travels through the country had taken me across wide rivers and into forests and mountain ranges. I had discovered great cities. All now seemed so distant.

My stomach growled. If this were tomorrow—when Mother expected me—she would have chicken, floured, salted, peppered, and ready to fry.

The seabag grew too heavy. I heaved it from my shoulder, resting it on the edge of the pavement. A car passed by, headed downtown. I recognized Pete Varneman. He had on the same old dark-framed glasses and khaki workclothes. He recognized me, too, but he didn't stop to say hello. Small town people have a way of knowing. I lifted the seabag, carrying it awkwardly like a suitcase until the aches had subsided and I again returned it to my shoulder.

A block from my destination all my physical burdens grew numb. Whatever smell of rain had greeted me was now gone. I moved forward without consciously walking. Recollections of high school parties and hurried assignments hung nearer than those of Cinderella liberties in distant ports.

A red-winged blackbird flew from the telephone pole to the white-cling peach tree behind Mother's clothesline. The same blackbird once eluded the BB's from my Christmas Daisy Repeater. I'd seen the same peach blossoms the day I left for the Navy. They'd not yet made way for the fruit. The wind shifted.

The grass under my feet needed mowing. I smelled wet stucco by the fresh-watered flower bed. The house asked me where I'd been. I took the two steps onto the porch. The seabag slid from my shoulders. A chocolate cake beckoned from the oven. I eased open the screen door. "Mother?" I whispered. "It's Alan. I'm home." A startled sound came from the kitchen. Across the dark living room, a gray-faced woman appeared in the kitchen doorway. Her lips were parted, her eyes wide. I tried to speak.

TWO

CHICKEN BONES piled up on my plate. Mother's face held back a thousand questions. Daddy was everywhere about the house. We'd talk about it in time. Throughout the meal, wordless sentences passed between us, separated by meaningless spoken ones. Through the open window a breeze again hinted of rain. It would be a night for sleeping under a quilt.

"I suppose this town will seem pretty dull to you now," Mother said.

"There's nothing dull about being home." I set my plate aside and stretched back in the chair. "The breeze feels nice."

"It was an early scorcher 'til the clouds came up."

Mother cut one slice of cake. For me. She had hardly touched her own food. It was not her meal. I found myself growing used to the extra lines and gray hairs. She seemed stronger. I'd been a "TK"–a teacher's kid, and, as such, watching my mother closely had become a habit. I'd wanted to see her through others' eyes. What did they see that I did not? What qualities that I saw were they unaware of? Mother had been teaching English to Brodie High students for fifteen years before her retirement. Before that she had been a substitute teacher, attending college part time on her meager earnings. A few of my fellow students had shared my experience of being in a parent's classes, but being in a parent's English classes–and for four years–somehow seemed a special challenge and, I was sure, enabled me to learn more about my own parent. In learning to reveal my view of the world through writing, I'd had my mother's guidance; in exploring the world through literature, I'd shared my mother's experiences and her insight.

"Do you miss teaching?"

Mother smiled. "Oh, some. Not during the day. I miss organizing the Halloween parties. That was fun. I miss seeing the children grow." Her face brightened. "For awhile, believe it or not, I even missed selling basketball programs."

"And how does it feel not getting up and going to work"

"The first weeks when I heard the loaded school busses coming through town in the mornings, I felt so down. I knew that I'd made a terrible mistake."

"And now?"

She laughed. "And now it's such a relief when I hear them, knowing that all that pressure is gone and my life is my own." Still smiling, she looked me straight in the eyes. "You know, I've never said this to you—I didn't want to be a pushy teacher mom—but I've often pictured you in front of a classroom. You'd be a wonderful teacher."

My smile was uncomfortable. "You've seen me in front of a classroom. I was always scared to death with everybody staring at me, ready to laugh if I made a mistake."

Mother reached across the table and patted my hand. "Don't worry. I'm not going to pressure you. You've got lots of time ahead of you, and you have your own mind. It's just that, by telling you how much I enjoy being retired, I don't want to turn you away from teaching. Besides," she said. "I've also pictured you in a lot of other professions—all very noble."

I was not ready to discuss—or even to think about—my future. Teaching was certainly a profession I had considered but not for my immediate future. If ever I were to become a teacher, I wanted much more life experience behind me. Mother had started her career years before my birth and then had reentered the profession after years of "real-life" struggle, but most of my teachers had never known another life. That was tradition. Like most of my generation, I felt that a new era had begun and that traditional approaches no longer were valid. And, besides, I wanted to hear more about my mother's life *now*.

"I bet you've caught up a lot on your reading."

"Oh, yes," she answered. "Actually, though, I've spent more of my reading time getting reacquainted with old friends. Some of those books I've been saving for my retirement will never get read, I'm afraid."

"I'll read them for you."

"You've probably already read some of them. Teaching public school, I suppose, has ruined me for all but the classics."

Yes, I might have read some of them–and many others on those long voyages at sea, one or two, of course, that I would have been ashamed to acknowledge. But, in addition, there had been novels not on my mother's list, some too new, some too angry. Social commentary had not been my mother's favorite, but the sixties was the age of nonfiction. Little had I expected that much of my spare time in the Navy would be spent exchanging and discussing books with my shipmates, but such had been the case. While, over the years, the faces continued to change, with most new faces gravitating toward the pinochle and poker games, always there were readers. Sometimes the least likely candidate would turn out to be the most avid reader and most able critic.

"You can't go wrong with the classics," I said.

"I haven't so far."

I glanced down at the few cake crumbs remaining on my plate. My stomach commanded me to stop eating. "The guys sure appreciated the cakes you sent. And I did, too. But I always remembered how good it is fresh-baked and iced."

Her eyes sparkled. "I'm cooking gingerbread tomorrow."

I touched her hand and smiled. "I should have called from the airport." My original plans had been to take a slow bus ride home, exploring cities I'd missed in my travels. But before I'd crossed the Mississippi, my bus ticket was cashed in and I'd hopped a plane to Lubbock and then caught another bus to Brodie.

"If you had called, you wouldn't have gotten any chocolate cake. I'd have been standing in the doorway the whole twenty miles you were on that bus home.

We laughed together, and in the pause that followed, I noticed the quiet. The curtains moved, but the breeze was silent. I could hear the house breathe. And the wind-up clock in Mother's bedroom.

"You know, the whole town looks different to me."

"Brodie? Why this town hasn't changed in thirty years."

"You haven't been gone most of the last four."

Mother's eyes grew distant. "Oh, I know what changes you're talking about. But it's no more than the different faces I saw each year in the classroom. Or the new fashions that the women try out from time to time. All you see different are the new faces and the new styles."

"I guess you're right," I said. "I guess the Brodie I knew is just out of style this season."

Mother's eyes came back to me. "My, you've done some growing up while you've been away."

"You mean I've lost some of the green around my gills?"

"Oh, yes. You may think I'm being a silly old mother, but it's a warm feeling for a mother to see her son turn into a man."

I returned Mother's smile, fighting for a brief moment the hurt of knowing I would never walk with my father as a man. But the moment was too precious for sorrow. "You look fine, Mother," I said. "This old town may have put on a new face, but as far as I'm concerned, you haven't changed a bit."

Mother, to my surprise, was embarrassed. "You don't think I'm getting old and ugly?" She laughed almost like a schoolgirl.

"You'll never be old to me. And the last thing you'll ever be is ugly."

Her laughter drained away. She looked down, and her face became radiant., "I'm glad you're home, Alan." The moisture shone in her eyes. My throat went tight, and the blood ran warm in my head. "Well," she said, standing up, brushing away the tide of emotion whose time had not arrived, "you should go to bed early and get a good rest tonight."

"I want to help put supper away."

"You go on." She was still smiling but persistent. "I'd like to be by myself a little while."

I wandered into the living room. Little had changed there. Daddy's ash stand still stood by the recliner; its polished glass liner gleamed with his absence. On top of the old upright radio was the fortieth anniversary portrait, moved from the bedroom they had shared. I turned the knob and the dial light came on, but I didn't wait to see if the old tubes still worked. Amos 'n' Andy and The Shadow lay asleep behind the grill cloth. From across the room the console TV stared in disdain.

This was the moment I had dreaded the most. Many times I had come home to find Mother alone in the kitchen while Daddy plowed late in the fields. Many times after my interest in fishing became marginal, I had eaten meals in the kitchen with Mother. Up to this point I had not allowed myself to face the reality of Daddy's passing, but in this room there was no denial. I closed my eyes and once again fought the coming emotions until the clatter of dishes in the kitchen caught my attention and allowed me to force my thoughts on the present.

A lone junebug buzzed the front screen. I went to the door and stepped onto the porch. Under the streetlamp at the corner, the grass and pavement were yellow. A streak of silver crossed the sky under a three-quarter moon. The breeze had died away, but the dampness lingered.

Taking off my shoes, I walked barefoot on the grass, feeling its limber blades sliding between my toes. A cold shiver rushed through my body and left me refreshed. Down the street, one window was lighted in the parsonage. I saw the darkness at David's window. The damp grass began to sting my feet.

I remembered a time at sea when the ship, nearing St. Croix, had sliced through a glassy sea. The orange moon on purple water had rolled like flowing silk in the wake, breaking and coming together in mercurial droplets. My mood had been like clear May nights of the past, totally absorbed in the here and now. But *here* and *now* my mood was of the past. And I could not feel the present *for* the past.

Mother was closing windows when I returned. "I'm going to leave a window cracked open a little in your room." she said. As she walked toward my bedroom door, I saw that her steps were slower and more deliberate. She had once glided easily from place to place. It occurred to me that her dress was on old-lady dress, her hair combed out of the way rather than styled. Still, she was strong and alert.

"I put an extra cover on the bed," she said as I entered the room. "It was down in the low forties last night." The corners were turned back, the sheets smooth, the pillows neatly in place. On the walls were pictures that had been moved from other rooms. A pincushion seemed at home on the dresser. It was not my room anymore; it was Mother's extra bedroom.

"This is gonna be the best sleep I've had in four years."

"Well, you just sleep 'til noon if you want." She walked to the doorway and turned back to me. She stood, staring. I couldn't read her expression. Going to her, I kissed her on the forehead.

"Sleep well."

"I will. Good night."

The room echoed with the quiet. Through the cracked window, night coolness seeped into the room. Many memories I'd left here. I closed my eyes. The memories came. Rounding the corner of the garage, I took David Brandon by complete surprise. "Bam!" I cried. "I got you." Clutching his belly, he dropped his submachine gun to the ground. "One life for my country," he moaned.

I opened my eyes. One life.

Images cast against the darkness of the room. Daddy's hand on my shoulder. Fear burning in my eyes as I spun to face him. "How 'bout lettin' me have a bite of that?" he asked matter-of-factly. I handed him the half watermelon, and he cut off a ring. "Don't worry. I already paid Carlos for it. You don't hide none too good." His eyes twinkled. "Now, how come you want to get into Carlos's patch when we got a whole garden full?"

I slept.

THREE

THE HORIZON beyond my morning walk stretched as straight and level as that of the sea. The water here, though, was rich brown soil and the waves, neat rows of fresh-plowed earth; the wave caps, tiny cotton and sorghum plants breaking through the crust and reaching upward, shining bright green in morning sunshine. Under my feet, the crushing of soft clods awakened long dormant memories; I hadn't realized the emotions such an ordinary experience could bring.

I'd forgotten colors. Even the brown of the soil seemed to glow. Three months in dry dock in a smoky city had dulled my sense of color. But here on the High Plains, soil, plants, sky, the old yellow Moline tractor plowing in the distance were brilliant.

In another field an irrigation motor growled like a contented Tom, and here and there across the landscape a tractor trailed a cloud of dust. Ahead and to the side I could see fingers of wet soil reaching across the fields. Small plants in the darkened, already damp ground beyond stood erect and proud.

Two miles behind me, the town and its white frame houses, its tin elevators and cotton gins shimmered in the early light. There was not a cloud nor a breeze. The damp threat of the evening before had disappeared with the darkness. Not a trace of pollution dulled the sky. Not a smell that was not natural reached the nostrils. To be sure, a windy day before the crops were up might fill the sky with dust and bring an unpleasant odor if one were too near a feed lot, but this spot lay over twenty miles from such an annoyance, and especially on a still day like today, sight and smell were pollution-free.

Zack's turn row ended at a pasture behind his work shed. Every worn-out implement and tractor he had ever owned had been neatly parked along the barbed wire fence. Rusty old breaking plows and harrows, with age-old tumbleweeds between their teeth, nestled among tall grass and weeds. Down by the corner of the pasture, a mostly wooden drill from the far-gone days of wheat farming rotted quietly away.

I'd expected to be trumpeted in by the barking of Zack's hound, but my intrusion had yet to be detected. Spider would probably be dead by now, but Zack would have another in his place.

The work shed remained in total disarray. In my fourteenth year Daddy had loaned me out out for a week to help Zack build that shed. The new wood had weathered to gray before the following summer. And now the structure looked older than the soil. Tools, plow points, nuts and bolts, welding rods, were scattered about with no logic. And Zack, I knew, could locate any item with his eyes shut.

The chicken house was being torn down. Beside the disassembled section lay an orderly stack of useless lumber. The barn itself leaned slightly southward, a tribute to forty years of blue northers, but the heavy eight-inch corner posts, though leaning, appeared undaunted.

Walking up to the fence, I peered over the top. A dozen or so mixed Hereford, Angus, and assorted dairy breed cows turned lazily toward me. A huge Hereford bull, the most purebred looking of the lot, was down and resting against the water tank, making things difficult for the several calves.

I recognized an old black, speckled cow walking toward me and remembered the day Zack had bought her as a heifer. She never grew much, sort of a lifetime heifer, yet her thin, bony frame had produced more than her share of fine offspring. Staring intently at my face, she walked to within five feet of me and stopped. I'd always been told that animals could not recognize faces. I returned her stare, but she didn't budge. Nor did she move as I turned to walk away.

Behind the abandoned windmill tower was the outhouse, its door latched from the outside. A hard dirt trail led around the tower, past the pressure pump enclosure to the screened back porch of the house.

The house itself was stark undashed stucco. A square structure, its wood-shingle roof slanted on four sides to an apex over the very center of the house. Off to the side, a garden flourished. Zack always had the first tomatoes of the season. I could almost taste the okra that I loved fried and Zack ate several ways, including raw. Like every farm house of the plains, Zack's was surrounded by a few brave windswept trees, mostly Chinese elms, making its acre or so an oasis on an otherwise unremarkable landscape. But as the crops began to grow, that impression would change.

"Well, I'll declare." Zack was rising from his rocking chair beside the kitchen table. Spider, curled up on a circular rug on the porch, raised sad old eyes to me. His tail came off the floor and dropped at painful intervals. I opened the screened porch door and reached down to scratch behind Spider's ears. His head pushed surprisingly hard against my hand. "I'll declare," Zack repeated. "Will you looky who's here. Come in, boy."

I rubbed Spider's head once and let him lick my hand as I stepped away. His milky old coat had grown wrinkled, the auburn and black spots dull and undefined.

"Hi, Zack," I said, reaching for his hand. His grip was firm. Putting both hands on mine, he stood back, looking me over. He still stood as tall as I, though his shoulders drooped more than I remembered. His khaki work clothes were faded but spotless, his eyes deep set, yellowed, with dark pupils; his hair, coarse gray-black. Above the hat line, the skin was pale, almost smooth. Below, it had been browned from many unprotected hours in the sun. The broad, hard features of his face came alive as he grinned.

"Sit yourself down," he said, motioning me toward an unpainted wicker-back chair. "I'll get you some coffee."

"Thanks," I answered, looking about the kitchen as I sat catching up on memories.

Zack took his lower front teeth from his shirt pocket and put them in place. He wore them only to talk and eat. I noticed no sweat marks on the back of his shirt as he turned to the stove to pour my coffee. He obviously had not been working.

Over his shoulder he said, "Talked to your mother yesterday. Told me you wouldn't get here 'til late this evenin'."

"Couldn't wait. Turned in my bus ticket halfway home and flew the rest of the way. Figured I'd seen enough countryside to last awhile."

"Well, I bet she was glad to see you."

"Had fried chicken floured and chocolate cake waiting."

"Yeah, she was glad."

"Your cotton looks good."

"Might get a stand." He set the steaming cup of black coffee on the table beside me. "Didn't get a late freeze this year." He returned to the rocker and put the cigar he'd been chewing back into his mouth. "Well, you out for good?"

"Yep."

"Don't reckon you'll be stayin' 'round here. Got any plans?"

"Nope."

Chuckling, Zack ran his thick fingers through his hair. I felt something soft and wet on my hand and looked down to see Spider. He sat down beside my chair and leaned his head against my leg.

"Guess you know about David."

"I know." A painful moment. Something we had to get over with. "I was at sea. They wouldn't let me come home."

"War's a terrible thing. I lost my brother in Italy."

"I know."

"A terrible thing," Zack repeated wearily. He stared off to the side of me. He'd been almost as close to David as to me, but I was sure that he was thinking of his brother now. I saw the wet cigar start to slip through his fingers.

"Well, you sure look like a busy man today," I said, a little louder than necessary.

"What?" He jerked his head toward me. The cigar fell anyway, but he didn't seem to notice. "Oh, yes. Guess I don't look much like a workin' man, do I? Fact is, the old tractor is in the shop, and I'm gettin' ready to go to an auction today. Old widow Macy's finally sellin' all her stuff and goin' to Florida. Wanta go with me?"

"No, this is my first day back. Guess I'd better spend it around home. Gotta get that old car of mine running."

"You mean you walked from town?"

"Wanted to. It's been a long time since I've had a chance to walk that far without touching metal or concrete."

Zack laughed. "Guess so," he said. "When you get ready to go back, I'll give you a lift."

"Okay." I drained the last swallow from my cup. "Better be soon, though. Got an idea Mother's fixin' a feast for dinner."

"And another for supper, I bet," Zack roared.

We both stood. Spider moaned as I walked away. He didn't follow. I patted him, but he knew I was leaving. He didn't try to lick my hand.

We left the door unlocked. The tree branches were bending to a slight wind now, but it didn't look like the dust would blow. It felt strange to get into the pickup and not see Spider springing up to the bed.

The dashboard was covered with everything imaginable: screws, can openers, matches, cigars. Bits of tobacco stuck to the metal everywhere, and tobacco odor dominated the interior of the cab. But it was a pleasant odor. Zack chewed his cigars; he never smoked them.

"You know," Zack said when we'd both settled in, "your mother offered to let me farm your dad's place."

"Yes. I wanted her to ask you."

Zack gazed over the steering wheel. "If I was younger, I would've. Me and my equipment's just a bit too far gone."

"We just wanted you to have the first chance." I knew that it had hurt Zack to turn it down. But I understood. Most of Daddy's 160 acres covered what we called a 'hill,' which sloped down to what we called a 'lake.' The hill was enough of a rise to make irrigation impractical on all but a few acres, too few to pay for the expense, and the lake was enough of a depression to collect rainwater from miles around. Wresting a decent living from one of the most difficult parcels of land on the High Plains had been too much for Daddy even when he was a young man.

The west border of Zack's land lay a half mile from the east border of Daddy's. Zack's house stood in the middle of a mile square section and was not served by a county road, though his two hundred or so acres bordered on two of the dirt roads that ran straight north and south or east and west exactly one mile apart all across the plains. Zack started the twenty-eight-year-old engine and we bumped down the turn row toward the also dirt county road. We would not pass Daddy's place, and I was glad. The rows going by the side window looked as though someone were thumbing across the leaves of a giant book. It was all so familiar. I'd never felt so far from the sea.

FOUR

I SAT ON the back steps, picking out a tune I'd made up on my guitar. Mother was taking an after-lunch nap on the sofa. I felt incredibly satisfied after the meal. Taste was another sensation I was rediscovering. The vegetables had all come from last year's garden, except for the collard greens Zack had given Mother. Her own garden by the back fence was in an early stage; a few weeks would pass before we would eat from it. After Zack dropped me off, I'd mowed the lawn. The sweet freshness of new-cut grass filled the air.

I thought of Daddy; it was impossible not to. His memory had become a book written by a dead author. Every tree that had been set out, every addition to the house and yard, almost, it seemed, every stick and stone held a reminder. Inside the house, it was only more so. All reminders, if I allowed myself to dwell on them, eventually led to the awful memory of the call to the chaplain's office, the medical descriptions, the hard, fast journey. And, so, I tried to keep my thoughts in motion. Coming home was painful—as I knew it would be. Quiet moments like this I found difficult, waiting to explode. And, yet, I craved quiet moments. I wanted to bring back—to touch again. But not to relive.

I lost track of the melody I'd been playing. Leaning the guitar against the house, I stood, trying to stretch the laziness out of my muscles. The garage, set back from the house almost to the alley, had been on my mind all day. I almost dreaded going inside.

The garage door was unlocked. Raising it, I was surprised to see everything so clean inside. Across the back wall was Daddy's and my workbench with tools carefully arranged on the pegboard behind. On one wall were lawn and garden tools, and on the other, rows of full and empty canning jars, the full ones placed there after the latest freeze, probably during Mother's thorough spring cleaning indoors.

It was a one car garage, and the one car it contained, a 1954 Chevy, was on blocks. Its metallic green paint had faded only slightly. The hubcaps were 'spinners' I'd once prized. The car hadn't been driven in three years, and the physics axiom came to mind: an object that is at rest usually wishes to remain so.

Taking a screwdriver from the pegboard, I pried off the hubcaps and stacked them under the bench. On the passenger side, the door came open with a pop. I'd forgotten that. The inside was musty but just needed airing. Except for a torn Lubbock street map, the glovebox was empty. I'd vacuumed and cleaned out the pre-Navy memorabilia before putting the car on blocks.

After opening the other door and the back windows, I went outside, leaving the garage door open behind me. The grill of Mother's five-year-old Ford in the drive grinned at me, as sparkling and clean as when it had been the new driver's ed car. Daddy's old pickup, mate in almost every way but color to Zack's, had been sold months before. Its absence was no special reminder during this hour, and, in fact, only on Sundays had occupied its spot alongside the curb during daylight hours.

I took the guitar inside the house and found my car keys where I'd stored them. Mother was still asleep as I passed through the living room to the front porch. The sun shone bright on the front lawn. Sitting on the steps, having somehow lost interest in my old car for the time being, I nursed the empty feeling of having and wanting nothing to do. After awhile, I went inside and left a note for Mother.

I walked quickly from the house toward downtown, feeling guilty for not stopping at the parsonage. But I wasn't ready for that.

Sparrows filled the trees. Dogs and cats roamed free but

generally kept to shady paths. Almost every house had a garden, and several were being tended. The subdivision atmosphere I'd grown accustomed to in cities was totally absent here. Long, brick ranch-style houses and small, white wood-frame structures existed side by side, along with a variety of other styles from a variety of eras. The wood and stucco houses that were not white were colored in light shades, and their roofs were low, with eaves extending a foot or more over the sides. Most of the houses were closed, with air conditioners humming at the windows. At one window a water cooler screeched noisily. The eighty-degree weather had come quickly, but most of the locals would soon become used to it and open their houses again, waiting for the high nineties.

Main Street traffic was fairly busy for a weekday afternoon. As I entered the downtown section, I noticed that the sidewalks, too, were busy. Almost all the people were tall and lean, with sharp features. One of the most vivid first impressions that Boston had made on me had been its relatively short and stocky population. In crowds, I had looked over the heads of most men and had experienced difficulty in buying clothes to fit. Here, I looked eye to eye with almost all grown males.

With few exceptions, the men were in workclothes, khaki or gray, but enough were in blue jeans that I didn't feel out of place. The women wore modest print dresses or slacks. Some of the younger kids were passing through on their way home from school. They carried lunch pails and Big Chief notebooks. The girls wore high-waisted, many-colored dresses. The boys scurried about with shirttails half in, half out.

I passed up the post office and the Brodie State Bank, both modern structures in comparison to their neighbors. The post office was light-colored brick with broad glass doors that revealed a wall of numbered boxes. The bank was fronted with blocks of blue marble veneer, with large aluminum lettering above the door.

Crossing a side street, Birch, I walked toward the Lobo Cafe. All the east-west streets were named after trees; the north-south streets, after cities. Main Street was Austin Avenue, but absolutely no one referred to it as such. All mailing addresses were post office box numbers, but all directions were given in relation to landmarks.

The Lobo Cafe had a new front. Window and door panes were shaded. As I entered, air conditioning sent a chill through my veins. The interior, too, was new, but the layout had not changed. I was mildly surprised to find a black man calmly eating at one of the tables. That had not been the case when I'd left for the Navy. Everyone seemed to know that it was coming soon, and, except for a few diehards, no one had been especially vocal about it. I had no illusions, however, that centuries-old attitudes had changed overnight.

Going to the counter, I ordered coffee. The waitress was an older woman, polite but not talkative. I didn't know her. The only other customer was a bread truck driver drinking coffee at a table by the window. During my high school years, it was a custom for junior and senior students to spurn cafeteria food and drive or walk to the Lobo two or three times a week for lunch. If I'd expected a nostalgia trip, though, it had not happened. Nothing inside that I could see was really changed, but there was no laughter. The place was little different from restaurants I'd known across the country. Finishing my coffee quickly, I left a small tip and the price of my purchase on the counter and stepped outside to welcome the warmth.

Across the street, through the pharmacy window, I thought I recognized Melinda Proctor. Or at least that had been her name when I left. I'd heard that she had married several years before. Melinda was a year younger than I and we had dated a couple of times in high school. But even though she was the first person I recognized from the high school days, I still was not ready to renew old acquaintances. I dreaded the thought of trying to recapture a time that was irretrievably gone.

Down the sidewalk, in front of each store, signs hung from the wooden awning that ran the length of the block. None were new to me, though two signs hung in front of now empty stores.

Sonny's Grocery and Market was at the center of the block. Several older men were on the bench outside the front window. I walked toward them.

Coot Rankin and L.C. were there and another man whose name I didn't remember. L.C. was a sometime employee of the feed store before I left home. Coot ran the scales at the Farmer's Gin, the lesser of the town's three gins, during the harvest season and sold worms the rest of the year. The other man did odd jobs. They all looked too old for work now. L.C. and the other man were toothless. Coot's remaining teeth were brown where they weren't yellow. His cough medicine bulged from a shirt pocket. All three were chewing tobacco.

"Afternoon," I said as I passed in front of them. Only L.C. looked up. He nodded without recognition. I was only one of many Brodie kids he'd seen grow up and leave the town and his memory. Coot and the other man were discussing world affairs, agreeing wholeheartedly with each other's wisdom.

Sonny's front door was open wide. He had no air conditioning, and I'd often wondered how it stayed so cool inside. The floors were bare unfinished wood, smoothed by decades of foot travel. The ceiling tiles were colorless. Even though there was a second story above, roof leaks had left many stains overhead. The front door opened between two large windows, with the square counter directly before it. A light film of dust covered the soft drink bottles, making cans and boxes and bags on display appear as though they had been there for years. Over the vegetable counter, straw hats were stacked—most western style but some Mexican sombreros. Sonny had almost all the downtown Mexican and Negro trade. On the opposite wall were the ice cream cooler and candy shelves. Everything was precisely the same. Everything except for the absence of Mr. Conner.

Sonny had taken over the store from his father when Mr. Conner suffered his stroke some twenty years before. I'd seldom been in the store when Mr. Conner's wheelchair was not there. There'd been a bare spot against the wall between the candy shelves and the fruit juice display where Mr. Conner backed his wheelchair out of the way. He was an alert man. He knew all the kids and teased them when they came by. The kids loved it. They'd stay to his crippled side when he'd try to reach out and tickle them. "Smart little bugger, ain't ya," he'd say. Then he'd wheel the chair around and grab them with his good hand. Only mops and brooms waited against the wall now.

I passed between the bread and pastry shelves and the patent medicines. The store was empty of customers.

"Whadaya know, Em'ly! Look who's comin' down that aisle." Sonny, behind the meat counter, wiped meat juice from his hands and came toward me. Emily rose from the desk off to the side of the meat section and followed. Over six feet tall, Sonny was lean and muscular. His hair was still black on top but almost white at the sides. Oldtimers still told of Sonny's basketball skills every time a new-generation star emerged.

"How are y'all doing?" I asked, reaching for Sonny's hand.

"Same as always," he answered, stepping aside for Emily. "Same as always."

Emily appeared from behind Sonny's frame. "We heard you were comin' home." Emily was short and slight, but she shook my hand vigorously. Her sand-colored hair was almost indistinguishable from the gray, making her appear to have aged little over the last several years.

"Got in last night," I said.

Sonny motioned. "Come on back. Tell us some sea stories."

I followed them back. Sonny returned to his meat cutting chores. Emily sat down by the desk, listening intently to the sea tales Sonny and I swapped. Sonny always told the same World War II Navy stories I'd heard all my life, but with each telling, the embellishments became more intriguing. From his tales, you'd think he had never seen action but he'd seen plenty.

Toward the front of the store I noticed the bread truck driver I'd seen in the Lobo, now in the process of exchanging old loaves for fresh ones. A young man about my age, he went expertly about his simple task. "Gotcha all fixed up," he called to Sonny when he'd finished.

"Hey-lo!" Sonny boomed back in his traditional greeting. "Got me fixed up, you say?"

"All fixed up." He came to the back and handed Sonny the ticket.

"Why doncha bring me some rain? We don't get nothin' but teasers here lately."

"Not in my department," the bread man said.

"Maybe that's the executive department," Sonny said, laughing. "Maybe one of these conventions comin' up will give us a president who can make it rain. Now that's the kinda candidate I could vote for."

"Well, it's not gonna be a Republican. That's for sure."

"Old Lyndon and his Democrats haven't brought us any rain," Emily teased.

"If they're smart, the Democrats'll run Wallace," the bread man countered. "They're stupid if they don't."

"What do *you* think?" Sonny asked in my direction. I didn't welcome the opportunity. As George Wallace's popularity had risen in recent months, I had anticipated confrontations back home like the one that seemed imminent. In an instant, I looked over the young man before me and saw what may or may not have been there. I saw a hero-worshipper, an undereducated, perhaps underintelligent man who wanted a president who would hold back or reverse the tide of progress in race relations. I saw a bigot.

"I don't think Wallace has a chance."

The bread man had accepted Emily's familiar teasing, but I was a stranger. He turned to attack. "You don't know how many people there are out there all over the country just waitin' for Wallace to get on the ticket. Shoot, they'll vote him in, all right. Them other candidates wanta pull out of the war. The people don't want that and Wallace won't let it happen. Even the people in them big cities up North. There's lots of workin' people just like me up there, and a workin' man will vote for Wallace."

"I just came back from Boston," I said, regretting my words before I'd finished, "and I didn't get that impression."

Suddenly, I was enveloped in silence. The bread man eyed me suspiciously. Silently, I accused him of being a draft evader. I ached to know what David Brandon had thought of the war as he walked into the minefield.

"There you go," Sonny said to the bread man, pretending to have missed the anger in my tone. "That kills that argument."

"Ah, Boston people are all liberals anyway," he said. "They're not like the rest of the people up there." With that, he took the ticket book and strode to the front door, calling over his shoulder. "You just wait 'til the convention." He picked up the basket of old bread and went out the door without looking back.

I could hear Sonny and Emily chuckling. Slowly, I recovered and wondered how long I'd been staring toward the front.

Sonny said, "Sure takes his politics serious."

"Yeah," I said, forcing a grin. I had the sudden desire to be somewhere else. I excused myself and left quickly.

As soon as I was outside, I took a deep breath. The bread truck was crossing the railroad tracks, heading toward the highway. Main Street traffic was unusually heavy. Two loaded school buses passed in front. Kids were everywhere—on the sidewalks and in cars. Already, high school kids had begun cruising up and down Main. Most of their cars were older heaps; some were the families' sedans, but a few were flashy sport coupes. I felt old.

I walked toward home, still angry at the bread man. Kids rushing innocently and noisily around me caught the overflow of my frustration. I needed to think, but their chatter and the roar of their engines crowded my mind. My background was strongly conservative, but a war thousands of miles away demanded answers to questions that were all too new. On shore patrol duty, I'd been in the middle of a Boston ghetto in search of stray sailors just before the fires started. I'd been in heated all-night discussions on many occasions far out to sea when the wind was still, the waves calm, and the only storms raging in the minds of street-tough kids from Newark, farmers' sons from Nebraska, and bright young men from all across the country. We knew how volatile was this decade; we knew that times were, indeed, 'a-changing'; we knew that people our age were a part of the change as perhaps never before. We were the bright young men of our age who for one reason or another had opted for the military for a time over college. I'd grown accustomed to an atmosphere in which people must express reasons for their beliefs and be prepared to defend them. I wanted to respect the bread man's opinion, but I could not overcome my anger at his use of the word 'stupid.' I thought of wonderful things I should have said.

The blurred image of a kid on his playful way home from school streaked across my path, followed by that of another whose careless pursuit almost sent us both tumbling. He never saw me, and I only saw the backside of his blue jeans and t-shirt and close-cropped brown hair as he scampered down Cottonwood Street after his equally oblivious companion. Ten years ago it would have been David and me.

FIVE

"I T'S A QUIET night," Mother said.

"Yes. It's nice."

She looked up from her book. The gold lettering on the faded blue cloth cover was visible only in spots. You had to look close to read the title: *Anthology of the World's Great Literature*. It had been with her since her freshman year in college.

"Mama used to say on a night like this that God was giving somebody a last peaceful hour with a loved one before he took him away."

At first, neither of us had mentioned death. Gradually, we were allowing death to take its natural place in our conversation. "That must have been scary," I said.

Mother leaned back in the recliner that used to be Daddy's and closed her eyes, thinking either of Daddy or of something she had just discovered in the book that she had been reading for forty years.

I lay on the sofa, engaged in a book on guitar chord progressions, one I'd been attempting to read for only two years. But my knowledge of music was too basic, my enthusiasm lacking. As much as I'd looked forward to coming home to rest without any immediate pressure, small chores that I really needed to tackle kept intruding on my thoughts. I'd been home one week and all that I'd accomplished was getting my old car to run and helping a little with the garden. I'd talked to Mother of going to school in the fall, but, for the moment, the thought of reentering college was unthinkable. I needed only two years or so, but choosing a major seemed like stepping into a bottomless pit. I thought of the flotsam I'd seen at sea serving no purpose to the world.

Mother's voice broke through the mists. "Are you going to graduation?"

"Graduation? When?"

"Tomorrow night. Didn't you know?" Graduation night in a small town was an event and, for Mother, especially so.

"Hadn't thought of it," I answered.

"You don't have to go. They'll expect me to be there. Of course, I want to go anyway. I had this year's seniors for home room last year."

"Maybe I'll just drive you over there."

"Oh, don't worry. I can drive myself. Or walk."

"No. I'll drive you."

She didn't answer. She was reading again from her book. It was opened to the middle, and I imagined that she was reading "Ulysses." The lines occurred to me:

How dull it is to pause, to make an end,
To rust unburnished, not to shine in use!

Through the open window came the steady hum of an engine as a car traveled past the house, the hum accompanied by the *click, click, click* of a pebble stuck in the treads. Closing my eyes, I strained to find what other sounds might be stirring in the night. Somewhere a radio was playing a rock-and-roll tune.

"I'm gonna take a walk," I said. Mother acknowledged with a glance and a smile. Tennyson had not intended his lines for her.

A million stars sprinkled across the blackness of the night. The moon was almost full, and the sky light, added to that from street lamps and lighted windows, cast a soft glow over trees and rooftops. Away from town, the same clear High Plains air that gave such vivid color to the day added contrast to the night sky.

I followed the sound of the radio.

No light shone in the parsonage, except from a window of Brother Brandon's study. Looking through the window at an angle, I saw against the back wall the huge shadow of the preacher bent over his desk.

The radio music came from a car parked by the Community Center a block off Main Street. It was an older model sport coupe, but its highly-waxed body gleamed in the half-light. The radio was not loud. A deejay hawked the latest collection of golden oldies. One boy sat on a fender and another stood close by, the red tip of a cigarette burning near one hand of each boy. I walked toward them, purposely moving heavily through the loose gravel to announce my approach. One of the bright red spots disappeared quickly behind the leg of the boy on the fender.

"Evenin,' fellows."

"Evenin,' " they both muttered. With my face visible and not a threat, I noticed the bold reappearance of the cigarette.

"My name's Alan Wilson. Do I know you two?"

"You're old la—. I mean, you're Mrs. Wilson's son, aren't you?" the standing boy said. I could see his blush even in the dim light.

I laughed. "Yeah, I'm old lady Wilson's son. Don't worry. She was my English teacher, too."

They both laughed politely. The standing boy easily matched my six feet. His smooth, youthful face was awkward over broad shoulders and angular frame. In a high school with little more than a hundred students, he was no doubt an athlete. The other boy was somewhat smaller, his face freckled, his hair short and parted low on the side. He wore cowboy boots and a wide belt with a large 'Texas' buckle.

"I'm James Stacy," the taller boy said. "That's Billy Atwood." I remembered James Stacy as a twelve-year-old.

"You boys graduating tomorrow?"

"I am," James said.

"I'm not. I'm just a junior," said Billy Atwood.

Six years earlier I would have fit right in with these two. Now, I looked from one boy to the other and realized that I had nothing to say to them. An overwhelming urge struck me to ask their opinions on the war. I wanted to know what they had felt when the news of David's death hit town. I wanted to hear that it had stirred people to thought. The six years since my own graduation had seen the world turn upside down. And, still, kids talked together innocently on a quiet May night, smoking cigarettes and feeling ill at ease in the presence of someone only a few years their senior.

"Do you have plans after graduation?" I asked James. It sounded to me like an adult-to-child question the moment I'd asked it.

He shrugged his shoulders, taking a nervous drag from his cigarette. "Mess around, I guess, 'til college starts. maybe get a job to earn my tuition money."

"Well, good luck." I smiled to him and nodded a 'good night' to Billy. Both appeared relieved at my departure.

Continuing on down the block, I found myself circling back to the house. I felt gravel through the soles of my shoes, night air at the back of my neck, well-worn jeans and chambray shirt clinging loosely to my skin. My eyes burned with a wanting to let something go. My limbs ached with a desire to strike out at the agonizing fear that David's brief life had served no purpose but to illuminate my own.

No lamps chased the darkness from the street I walked. The houses were black and silent, the pavement uneven. I turned and found myself running back in the direction from which I'd come, out from under the trees that shielded the street from the stars and moon. I ran beneath the water tower, past the Little League park, the Boy Scout house, and the fire station. Crossing the last paved street, I ran through a vacant lot, slowing down only to step across the single set of railroad tracks. I was in the gin yard, surrounded by empty cotton trailers. Sitting down heavily on the tongue of one, I tried to catch my breath. My arms and hands glistened in the moonlight. My clothes stuck like paint, and my heart thudded painfully. Climbing inside the trailer, I lay back on the hard surface.

Nearby highway sounds died away. I stretched out under the

stars just as I had that night on the flight deck off the island of St. Thomas, not knowing that David was dead. It had been a peaceful night. Lights from Charlotte Amalie blinked up and down the hillside. Waves lapped against a sleeping bow, and the giant ship moaned and creaked to the tune of gentle swells.

SIX

THE MORNING of graduation day the the grind and clatter of Mother's washing machine and dryer drove me early from the house. The sun was warm. It was a lazy day. Women tended flower beds, deliberately but effortlessly weeding and watering. The times I'd worked Mother's garden, I had always ended up sweaty and dirty. But the ladies today might as well have been knitting in the shade for all the perspiring they did.

Downtown, I ordered coffee at the Lobo and sat next to the window with the *Lubbock Morning Avalanche.* War and presidential politics dominated the headlines, straining my mental pact to sidetrack those subjects for awhile. But the Wallace bumper stickers and talk of Nixon or Reagan actually enticing the county away from its Democratic tradition proved difficult to ignore. Humphrey looked like a shoo-in for the Democrats, and I just couldn't imagine his taking many votes from the khakied, weather-faced crowd in the Lobo.

Across the street, the broad pharmacy window glass was stained like a medicine bottle. Sunlight reflecting off the surrounding yellow bricks thwarted a view inside.

The talk around me was loud, friendly, and argumentative. Customers seated at two tables talked from table to table and among themselves. First, next season's high school football team; then, fishing; then, a variety of farm-related topics. Men and women alike gossiped unashamedly. Nothing that had passed down Main Street in twenty years had escaped their attention. I felt naked in their presence and sublimely secure.

I left the newspaper in the cafe and crossed the street to the pharmacy. Curiosity guided me through the door. If it really had been Melinda I'd seen inside that day, I was now anxious to find how time had changed her.

Inside, the pharmacy was cool and incredibly quiet. Antiseptic mediciney odors permeated the place. Neat, tedious rows of tiny bottles covered one wall, and pink and blue cosmetic colors adorned another. From behind the partition separating the pharmaceuticals from the less protected wares came subdued voices. Meanwhile, I scanned the counters, wondering what I'd say when one of the voices confronted me.

"Good morning, Sir."

I turned to see a white-smocked, middle-aged man peering around the partition.

"Morning," I answered.

"We'll be right with you."

I reached for a can of Band-Aids, just in case I needed support, and waited. Melinda appeared a moment later, nicely manicured and wearing an attractive but simple dress. I noticed the ever-so-slight lines around the eyes, the gently curling shoulder length hair a shade lighter than I had remembered.

"Why, hello, Alan."

I put the Band-Aids back in place. "Hi."

"I heard you were back in town." I was amazed that I'd never before noticed her soft Southern accent. "I hoped you'd stop and say hello." The years became more apparent as she stepped closer. If I'd seen her up close that first day, I might not have recognized her.

"You've been hidden behind these stained windows," I said.

"Excuses, excuses." I suspected that she felt as awkward as I.

"I really didn't expect to find anybody around from the high school days."

"Oh, there are a few of us still around. Ken and Margie from your class and Francine Nelson from mine. She's Francine Smithers now. Carl Bascom was in your class, wasn't he?"

"Yes."

"He's still around."

I could hear the pharmacist shuffling bottles behind the partition, and I grew a bit nervous, wishing for privacy.

"I'm staying with the folks awhile," Melinda said. "The girls and me. I've been working for Mr. Woodward two months."

She smiled. "Melissa—she's three-and-a-half. And Sandra. Sandra's two."

"Time gets by."

We talked a few minutes longer until a customer came in asking for assistance, and I left after promising to give her a call. I'd learned that her name was now Aldredge. I tried it out in my mind, but it didn't seem to mesh.

I felt odd walking home. A block away, I made a detour, turning back toward the railroad line and the highway and walking down the street parallel to the tracks where they cut through the Mexican part of town. At the first pink stucco house, the pavement ended abruptly. Mariachi music hovered over the grassless yard. Mexican hillbilly, Manuel used to call it. On the wooden front porch, a loosely-diapered baby struggled with a rubber ball too large for her grasp. A transistor radio hung by a strap from the only tree in the yard. From underneath a rusted-out old Dodge pickup on blocks, two legs protruded, straining in concert with the screech of a bolt reluctantly giving way to the wrench.

Manuel had been the only Mexican-American male of the twenty-two members of my graduating class. Occasionally I'd eaten with his family. Fluffy flour tortillas folded over refried beans and chopped peppers. Tangy menudo that made you ignore its uncamouflaged ingredients. All sorts of vegetable dishes that I didn't recognize and couldn't pronounce when I asked their names. Mrs. Hernandez always displayed a proud toothy smile when I complimented her cooking, but she never had anything to say except to the kids in Spanish. For fifteen years I suspected that she couldn't speak a word of English, but I never knew for sure. I did know that traditional Mexican meals were not the only meals the Hernandez family ate, but they were

Mrs. Hernandez's special meals and were always served when I visited. The last I heard of Manuel, he was driving heavy construction machinery down in the Rio Grande Valley. While I was in the Navy, the rest of the family made a harvest trip to California and never returned.

The Mexican section stretched a quarter mile down the wide dirt street. One set of well-traveled tire tracks wound their way around pock marks and deep ruts. Two identical new but small brick houses, basic modern structures without garages, fronted the street. Foliage and pretty, brightly colored flowers surrounded a few of the older homes.

Crossing a weedy vacant yard to the railroad tracks, I stood between the rails, the highest spot of ground in town, taking in the heavy odor of newly-creosoted crossties. Over beside the highway walked two sandled and robed figures, bearded and stooped Biblical fashion, not even drawing a glance from the employees of the butane company. Cars and trucks whistled past them, and the only evidence of their existing in the same world was a slight rustling of the men's robes with each encounter.

I walked farther down the track and turned back into town on the street leading past what its inhabitants called 'the flats' and most whites called something else. The aroma of barbecue filled my nostrils and made me suddenly hungry. Its smoke rose from somewhere just beyond the Baptist church. The black section of town was little different from the Mexican section except that most of the houses had some kind of livestock pen behind, mostly for pigs and most now vacant. A few hens roamed the streets, adding to other touches of permanence that contrasted with the Mexican houses.

The source of the smoke was a two-room shanty, a rusty old Nehi sign its only marking. I stepped over the falling-down hogwire fence and went to the screen door. A graying, squatty black man glanced at me as I entered. He was talking to an old black woman in a long beltless and sleeveless dress. The armholes, much too large for her skinny limbs, exposed her bosom each time she moved. The man expertly carved a charred hunk of fatty meat and wrapped it in white paper. Meat juice shone on his hands. And the same black soot that covered the barbecue pit, the walls, the floor, and everything near them was smeared with the grease marks on his apron.

The old woman's eyes followed him with quick movements, as though he were a naughty child trying to get away. "I want some pork too," she commanded.

"Ain't got no po'k"

"What you say?"

"I say I ain't got no po'k today."

"Well," she said, slowly unwinding a bill from her coin purse. "I guess I get some tomorra."

The man counted her change from a cigar box and handed it to her with the package. She took it wordlessly and walked to the door.

"Thank you, Ma'am. Come back," he called mechanically as the door closed behind her.

"What can I do for you?" he said to me, wiping his hands on his apron and putting the cigar box away.

"Just a pound of beef, I suppose. I wanted a pound of pork, too, but I guess you're out."

"What makes you think I'm out of po'k?" he asked dryly. He opened the pit and took out another hunk of meat, setting it beside the other. "You like it ma'bled?"

"A little."

"Outside cut?"

"That's fine."

He cut both pieces quickly, weighing them on his crude scale and adding the shreds to make the weight come out. He did not explain his reluctance to sell the pork to the previous customer, and I supposed that she had annoyed him in some way.

"Anything else?"

"Sauce. A pint if you've got it."

"Have to add to it some. Don't think I got that much." He went to a gas hot plate and stirred the extra ingredients into the bubbling red liquid in a sauce pan. I could see that he kept his body between me and the sauce, no doubt to keep his recipe secret.

"Is it hot?"

"Oh, yessuh."

"That's good."

The other room was not occupied. It had one wooden table covered with a yellowed oilcloth and an assortment of chairs—no napkins or condiments.

"How long have you been here?" I asked. "I don't believe you were here when I moved away."

"Two years," he answered, his bold features breaking into a grin. "You're the schoolteacher's boy, ain't you?"

"Word gets around."

"It's a small town." He laughed. "Oh, lordy. I've lived in lots of towns. Big'uns and little'uns. These little'uns, they all alike."

"Same as the big ones?"

"Hey, you right about that," he roared. "I been all over this country. Baltimore, Seattle, Houston—all over. Man, you can't find a dime's worth of difference nowhere."

He placed the two meat packages and the covered paper cup of sauce in a shoe box. I paid him and walked straight home, the warm box under my arm.

To be sure, Melinda was on my mind. Not that I wanted to get very involved. I had gathered from our conversation that she was now divorced—or, at least, separated from her husband. We'd had fun during the few times we'd spent together in high school, but we'd shared no special relationship. The mature Melinda I met today, however, was not the sixteen-year-old I had known, and I realized that I was no longer an eighteen-year-old looking for a date for the weekend. Besides, I'd not yet come to grips with a more recent relationship, and that was also very much on my mind.

A lot, in fact, was on my mind. Decisions about my immediate future had to be made. If my decision were college, preparations would be necessary, and, in fact, inquiries about application deadlines and such had already been made. I'd even considered going to work for a year or two using my Navy electronics training. Much could be said for that idea. It was still wartime, and the demand for electronics skill was high,. And I enjoyed the work. It would certainly give me time to comtemplate my future.

Or I could travel. One place in particular was on my mind. In Puerto Rico, on the highway from Roosevelt Roads to San Juan, there is a village surrounded by sugar cane fields. Across the highway is a mountain, green and fertile to the peak. The village itself is on the ocean shore. From the bus I'd seen beaches fifty yards wide bordered with natural palms growing close and tall like the pines of East Texas. It had been off limits because we had little time in port and could go only where the special bus went. From the window, it had been as far away as I felt it now walking home.

But this interval unfold by my own design, a lazy summer. If I traveled at all, it would be to visit a college campus. Or it would be an unscheduled, unplanned excursion to who knows where. Regimentation was too close behind. I needed barbecue and morning walks and sitting on the back porch, playing my guitar for the cornstalks and the marigolds. I could catch up to the future when the time came.

SEVEN

T
HE BARBECUE and I arrived home just in time to save Mother from preparing lunch. I had decided against going to the graduation ceremony. Somehow it seemed to be one of those meaningless duties that I didn't want to face. Mother didn't appear surprised. She insisted on walking to the high school, but I insisted on driving her home. When she left, it was with the aspect of a teacher, glowing with pride in her former students' accomplishments.

For the first time since my return, I found myself confronted alone by this place that had been the center of my world for most of my childhood. At first, I wandered about the house, remembering pleasantly a picture frame I'd given Mother for a birthday, a set of Grollier's Encyclopedias whose purchase (for my benefit) had caused a financial strain on the family. As hard as I tried, though, to avoid any painful reminders of my father, the effort proved impossible. Eventually, I gave in and allowed myself to feel his presence in what remained of him here in this house. As long as I did not give in to the temptation to remember or to try to relive, I could hold back the flood.

This was the first house that Daddy had ever lived in that was not in the country, and the adjustment when we moved in had not been easy. His work in the fields gave him little leisure time at home, but in the first few months here, I felt that he was staying at the farm a little longer than necessary. He just could not adjust to life in town surrounded by neighbors. He needed space. He needed to see his cows, his crops, and they needed his oversight.

What had saved him was the physical condition of the

house. Mother's new teaching job and the fact that the house needed repairs were the only reasons that the purchase had been possible. And if there was one thing Daddy approached with almost the same enthusiasm that he felt for farming, it was carpentry. In slack times when he could be away from the farm, he threw himself into house repairs and upgrading. Because of expenses, some jobs took years, and, in one two-year stretch, crop failures put a halt to all projects. Working on the outside of the house and the yard eventually brought him into a more comfortable contact with his neighbors, and Daddy liked his neighbors because he liked everyone. In the beginning, I had been Daddy's gopher, but as I grew older and learned, my contributions became more significant. Mother, it seemed to me, knew everything there was to know about decorating inside and gardening outside. By doing so much work on this place, we had become a part of it. With the remodeling and repairs complete, Daddy had started taking on paid carpentry work in those opportune periods.

I felt myself sinking toward that moment that I did not want to face alone. Closing my eyes, I whispered, "Not now. Not now." I did not want to run out; that was what I had been doing since I'd returned. Instead, glancing around, I searched for something to hold onto.

On the living room bookcase, I spotted the chronological row of Brodie High School yearbooks, predominately dark blue with white lettering, with a sprinkling in the reverse and one daring gray with blue lettering. There were two numbered '1962,' my senior year, one for me, one for my parents. I couldn't remember whether all the other yearbooks were considered mine or my parents', but it didn't really matter. The only one I wanted was my senior book, and I wasn't really sure that I even wanted that now.

Slipping that book out, I slowly fanned through the pages, intentionally beginning after the senior photos so that I would not encounter that of David. The world in those pages bore no resemblance to the world I had known since. Its theme was innocence. Now, every newspaper, every magazine, every news broadcast blared protests against the values and the lifestyles that book epitomized. I couldn't believe that we, the children in those photographs, deserved that onus. But, at the same time, I found it difficult to believe that we had been so very innocent.

In those pages, boys were football players who studied vocational agriculture; girls were cheerleaders and pep squad members who studied home economics. The most desirable of the boys were designated as 'heroes'; and, of the girls, as 'sweethearts'. In this first-to-twelfth-grade publication, fifty-four Hispanic faces graced the first grade section, but with each higher grade level, the numbers dwindled until only two were featured with the graduating seniors. No blacks appeared anywhere in the book. The black elementary and junior high school students received their schooling in used-up structures removed from the white neighborhoods. Black high school students were bused out of town. We knew all that, but what did we do?

I returned the book to the shelf, but before releasing it, I pulled it back. After a moment's hesitation, I opened the sophomore pages. The Melinda Proctor I knew smiled back at me. This Melinda did not know what lay in store for her during the next six years. Would her smile have been so alive? I closed the book.

She would be at home now, with her parents and her children. Dinner would probably be over. Perhaps, she'd be getting her children ready for bed? This was something I'd not dealt with. I wanted to call her. But, instead, did I really want to call someone else two thousand miles away, and was Melinda a convenient substitute? I told myself no; that relationship had ended months ago, and when I had boarded the bus in Boston, I was not thinking of *her* and was, in fact, surprised that I did not do so until the bus had left the city.

I picked up the phone. Mr. Proctor answered. Melinda was giving her girls a bath and would call me back.

To fill time, I went into the kitchen to make some coffee. While the coffee dripped, I tuned up my guitar and started into an old Hank Williams song called "Weary Blues from Waiting," one that had been a favorite of Daddy's. Why I started with that song, I didn't know. I'd gotten away from country music in the last few years.

The phone rang while I was pouring my coffee.

"Hi," Melinda said. "Mother said you'd called."

"Yeah. Thought I'd find out if that really was you I talked to today."

"Well, yes it was. Did I look that different?"

"As a matter of fact," I answered, "you did. You have to remember that you were only about fifteen or sixteen years old the last time I saw you."

She laughed. "And now I'm wrinkled and gray?"

"I sure didn't see any of that," I said. "I thought you might have gone to graduation tonight."

"I thought about it. Right now, though, I'm not sure I want to talk to a lot of people." She suddenly sounded weary. "People always have questions."

"Well, I don't have questions. I'm just looking for a friendly voice." We talked for another twenty minutes until it was nearing time to drive Mother home from graduation. Several times it occurred to me to ask Melinda out sometime over the coming weekend, but each time I hesitated. I was somewhat relieved when Melinda mentioned that she would be visiting relatives with her parents. But I did grow very comfortable talking to her, and I was very much reminded that she was no longer the teenaged girl of nineteen sixty-two.

As I drove to the school, I remembered a shipmate who had ended a relationship with a divorcee with children. "She was just carrying too much baggage," he had said. Melinda had not asked for my sympathy, but, though I knew virtually nothing about her situation, I couldn't help feeling for her and for any woman in her situation. For the time being, I would offer to be her friend and let it go at that.

Cars were parked everywhere within two blocks of the high school, but I managed to find one overlooked space behind the

Abandoned Highway

tennis court. Walking toward the entrance, I felt that at any moment I would be stampeded by exiting graduates and families. But the ceremony was obviously running a little longer than usual. I looked at my jeans and sport shirt and, only a little self-conscious of being underdressed, I strolled on inside.

Down the hallway the two auditorium doors were open and I could hear the commencement address still in progress. One boy and one girl, dressed in their finest commanded each doorway—honor society members as I recalled. A small table with graduation programs stood near each couple. I went right up to the nearest door, startling the girl there, who looked at me and then to the programs. I held up my hand to signal no thank you and walked on in.

It was standing room only. I leaned against the very back wall. In nineteen sixty-two, I would have been the only person in jeans, but I could see that times had become a bit less formal. Though few males wore jeans, many wore something other than suits. The most striking differences were in the appearance of the graduating class on the stage, especially the three black faces. The majority of the boys looked much like those in my graduating class, though several sported hair as long as that of the girls.

As the speaker finished his address and the principal strode to the platform to begin conferring degrees, I scanned the audience until I spotted Mother sitting with several other women whom I knew also to be retired teachers. This was an important time for Mother and I watched her, rather than the graduates, as the names were read and the graduates came to accept their diplomas. She beamed at the reading of each name, but I could tell that certain names were special.

Surely these graduates were not so innocent as I and my classmates had been. Surely, four years after the Gulf of Tonkin incident, the boys had been made aware of the danger of being *this* age at *this* time. Surely David's death had shattered any illusions they might have had. Surely the struggles for civil rights, for the rights of women, for abandoning old and sometimes meaningless traditions had challenged their minds.

When all degrees had been conferred and the class president had given the benediction, I found myself mumbling the words to the alma mater. And then it was "Pomp and Circumstance" and the graduates were flowing orderly but hurriedly off the stage. All around me families and friends clapped, cheered. Flashbulbs popped. Graduates, glowing, crying, rushed passed me into their futures.

As the last graduate fled past, I remained in place, watching as the crowd stood and turned toward the exits. Many faces I recognized but no one looked my way. It was as though I were a visitor from the dead, invisible to all around me.

Mother was in one of several clusters near the stage. I waited until she had finished her visiting and was walking alone. The last thing I wanted was to be reintroduced to old acquaintances. I chided myself for being so antisocial, but that malady had struck me since my return every time something had prompted me to remember the past.

Mother almost walked past, noticing me at the last moment. "Why, Alan. I nearly didn't see you." She looked at my jeans.

"I know," I said. "I'm not appropriately attired."

"Well, you weren't the only one," she said. "I don't know what the world is coming to." But she was laughing as she spoke.

We made our way through the crowd and to my old Chevy without being stopped for conversation. The door popped as I opened it for Mother and I made a mental note. We joined a stream of headlights and taillights, watchinng the graduates' cars peel off the procession and head for the community center for their commencement party. It was a beautiful May night, full of celebration, full of promise, and I, too, wondered what this world was coming to.

Four consecutive university semesters a hundred miles north followed my own Brodie High graduation. Then came the Navy. I'd broken the news to Mother during the Thanksgiving break, 1963. The following February I would leave for boot camp in San Diego. It was not a propitious time for making such an announcement. Our president had been assassinated only days before, but she had to be informed of such a consequential and imminent change of plans, consequential for the both of us.

"Why Alan!" Mother had responded, "Aren't you going to finish your degree?"

"In time," I said. "I just don't feel ready for upperclass courses now." During those four semesters I'd met a number of older students, most of whom were attending on the GI Bill. They were the ones who asked the most compelling questions in class. They were purposed; college was not a 'fling'. While I floundered in deciding my impending choice of major, they'd had years of realworld insight to draw on. Many, perhaps most, began their university careers with that decision in hand. And the fact that the veterans among them also had that GI Bill 'in hand' clinched it for me.

I had enlisted with an electronics school training guarantee, so after boot camp, my assignment was Electronics Technician 'A' School, Naval Station Treasure Island, California. The choice derived from no ambition for a career in electronics, but the field surely had the future in tow. Talk about a backup job skill! And the 'job skill' motivation dominated my fellow students' reasons for enlisting in the first place. Of course we were patriotic, willing to 'go to war' if that's what it all came to; after all, we were the children of combat veterans. We hadn't played cowboys and Indians — we had played world war combat. But we had joined a military with no major conflict looming. Insignificant little countries like Laos and Vietnam, with the aid of U.S. 'advisors', were keeping the commies from dominoing across Southeast Asia — jungle skirmishes that that had nothing to do with us! Then came the news flash from a faraway, previously unknown place called the 'Tonkin Gulf'.

EIGHT

"I'LL DRIVE you home," I offered.

"That would be nice."

Melinda sat all the way over against the passenger window of my old Chevy. Even with the space between us, her femininity stirred me with surprising intensity. I would not have called her a Madison Avenue beauty; her eyes were noticeably small, her shoulders, a little too narrow. But her skin was soft and her movements delicate. She had a pretty face and a slender build that gave her appearance a certain character that too much perfection might have destroyed. In other words: she was really cute.

"How was your day?"

"Inventory," was all she answered.

"Sounds tiring."

"Just tedious. It's a relief to have it behind us."

"How'd you like to go for a drive? If you're up to it after working all day."

"I'm fine," she said. "What did you have in mind?"

"We might make it to Silver Falls before dark if the old engine doesn't sputter."

"That does sound inviting." Though we had not kept in touch over the years, Melinda was still a friend. The two dates we had had in high school had been casual and had resulted in no more than occasional phone calls and good times in the company of friends.

We drove to her parents' house, and I sat in the living room with Mrs. Proctor while Melinda changed. It had been years since I'd waited with a parent for a date. Mr. Proctor, the assistant to the local postmaster, was not at home, and I would have been a bit more comfortable if he were. A friendly, familiar male visage would be welcome in this, currently, houseful of females. And in a small town, few faces are more familiar than those of post office employees. Mrs. Proctor was all smiles. Her daughter, she said, hadn't been getting out enough lately. The girls eyed me from behind the hallway door. Their grandmother couldn't coax them out. When I looked toward them, they ran.

Melinda came out wearing cotton pants and a plaid blouse. The girls trailed behind, clinging to her legs. "You kids stay with Grandmama," she said.

As I stood waiting, I could see their sad, pouting faces directed to the floor but staring up at me. I felt like Simon Legree.

"I don't think your daughters like me very much," I said while opening the car door for Melinda. She laughed, but I was sure that she hadn't understood.

It was a thirty-mile drive to Silver Falls. We listened to the radio and chatted. She wasn't as close to the window as she'd been earlier, apparently uncertain whether I had intended the outing as a date or as a casual drive.

"I remember when you used to sit closer to me," I said, glancing toward her, catching her smile.

"Is that another invitation?" she asked coyly.

"What do you think?"

We drove through Ralls, past other memories. Again, I saw change. But with Melinda beside me and the cool plains wind blowing through the window, I relished in the familiarity of it all.

Between Ralls and Crosbyton, Melinda pointed out the ruins of the Big Chief Drive-in Theater. The concession stand was intact, and headless speaker poles stuck up above the grass. The theater had been abandoned years before I was old enough to drive to it, but it had been a special place because Mother and Daddy and I had seen many movies here together. "I can almost smell the popcorn," I said.

"I remember the hot dogs," Melinda said.

"Come on, now. You're not old enough to remember."

Melinda gave me a light-hearted slap on the shoulder. "And you're not that much older than me, Alan Wilson. I was at least seven when it closed, and those hot dogs were dripping with mustard and chili."

"Okay, okay. It's just that sweet, innocent face that had me fooled."

"Just drive on," she responded.

"And all Texas hot dogs are dripping with mustard and chili," I teased, eliciting another slap.

We continued on, silently for awhile. Occasionally, we caught each other's eyes and exchanged a smile. As we traveled through Crosbyton, I turned to point out a cafe where we'd sometimes stopped with our classmates after ballgames. Melinda's eyes were shut. "Are you okay?" I asked.

She turned, slowly. "I'm fine." Again, I as struck by the soft accent.

"You are tired, aren't you."

"No, just thinking."

"Do you want to talk about it?"

"Yes. Yes, I want to talk about it, but I don't know how."

For the first time in about seven years, I took her hand in mine. "All you have to do is start saying what you feel. Remember that I'm your friend."

For a moment, she didn't respond, and I thought that she would close her eyes again. And then she said, "I want you to be my friend." She searched. "I mean, I want you to stay my friend. I just don't know what kind of friendship I want, and I don't know what kind you want." She hesitated and I sensed embarrassment in her choice of words.

I wanted to answer, to relieve her discomfort, but I, too, found myself having difficulty with the words. "I understand," I said. "My life, too, is kinda in limbo right now." I squeezed her hand. "I just really enjoy being with you."

"Thank you," she said, and I could hear the relief in her voice. "I really don't know why I'm saying all this. Here you've been nice enough to ask me to go for a pleasant evening, and I'm laying this heavy stuff on you."

"Lay it on," I said.

"I just hope I didn't sound—weird." Once more, the stumbling for words. "It's just that this is the first time I've been out since the divorce. And—like they say—it's a big step. It feels a little strange. And—and when you came into the pharmacy, well, it's just that sometimes you wonder what a guy has in mind."

I tried a reassuring laugh with little success. "I was feeling lonely and sorry for myself," I said, "and suddenly there you were."

She obviously tried to match my effort. "And so you decided that the first girl who came along would be just the one?"

"Yes," I answered, "and how incredibly lucky I was that it was you."

"Don't be so sure," she said with a smile. She placed my hand back on the wheel. "You might want to stay away from this gal."

"Not this evening, I don't."

Again she was silent, but this time without the tenseness. We were out of Crosbyton now and again surrounded by cotton fields. Melinda might have been idly gazing out the window and the passing scene. I suspected that she was unaware of anything but her thoughts. After awhile, she asked, "Aren't you just a little curious about my marriage?"

"Curiosity is one of my failings."

"Good. I'd be disappointed if you hadn't wondered about it." We exchanged another glance, and I could see that, though she was as uncomfortable about it as I, it was something that she needed to say. "You see," she began, "I'm old-fashioned about honesty. And I want you to know that, even though we may just be two old buddies out for one little drive together and nothing else, I wouldn't be here with you if I were still in love with someone else."

I looked at her again, but she didn't raise her eyes to meet mine. "I'm sorry that you've had unhappiness," I said.

"Oh, don't think about that."

"How long have you been divorced?"

"Six months—almost exactly as long as he's been remarried. We were separated when Sandra was born."

Again I took Melinda's hand. "You *have* had unhappiness," I said. "And I'm sorry."

"But—" She hesitated. "But I don't want you to think I'm bitter or anything. It was as bad for him as it was for me, and I really hope he's happy now."

"Does he ever come to see the girls?"

"No. He's never seen Sandra. And it's better that way. At least for now." She squeezed my hand and smiled up to me. She truly did not look bitter, and I wondered how she could not be. "Okay," she said, "now that all that is out, tell me about yourself. You must have been all over the world while you were in the Navy."

"Well, no," I answered, still struggling with my new-found anger at Melinda's ex-husband. "I did cover the country pretty much, though. And a few Atlantic and Caribbean islands."

"I've never been out of Texas."

"You can go a long way without getting out of Texas."

"We went to the coast on our honeymoon. To Galveston."

"Well, see there. You've got me on that one," I said. "I've never been to Galveston."

The West Texas caprock remained among the most abrupt terrain changes I had ever encountered. The land extended almost tabletop-smooth to the last yard before dropping into the canyon. Water and millenniums of wind had eroded away unimaginable tons of earth and rock, leaving a rugged and rolling canyon floor gutted by dry creek beds and decorated with buffalo grass, prickly pears, live oak and bushlike mesquite trees. But, after the recent rains, the earth was moist and the grass pleasingly green. A trickle of water ran down each gully. Evening sun brightened a myriad of wildflowers, in spots carpeting the canyon floor, yellow in one direction, light purple in another. It was not a place for delicate bluebonnets and Indian paintbrushes. Flowers here blossomed on hardy plants, some thorny, some with leaves almost white, but others on dark, pretty green plants that belied their semi-arid surroundings. Visitors in another season would be amazed to know what they had missed.

Silver Falls was a roadside park built alongside a six or eight foot fall of the White River. I'd ridden there on a hayride in high school. It was a spot for church and school picnics and a cool resting place for travelers.

The sun was low over the caprock when we arrived. Long shadows of evening extended from picnic tables and boulders. We parked away from the only other car and went down the rock steps to the river—actually more like a creek, and a small one at that. Usually clear, it normally spanned only ten to fifteen feet, though today it was a bit muddy and had swelled to maybe twenty or twenty-five. Its milky-brown water ran swiftly around a rocky bend, splashing noisily against low-hanging bushes. The falls were quieter than usual, though; with the river swollen from the recent rains, the drop was not so great. The usual trails were all under water, so we settled on a rock step halfway up the bank.

"Maybe if I'd seen some places you've been," Melinda said, "this wouldn't seem so pretty. But it still looks pretty to me."

"To me, too," I answered. "Niagara may be more impressive, but this is prettier."

She drew her knees up under her chin. "I'd like to see Niagara Falls."

"You should some day."

She smiled, staring off into the water.

"Shoot," I said, "I bet you think I'm trying to sound like the world traveler."

"I just envy you. That's all."

"It's different, though, when you see places in uniform. One of these days, I'd like to see it all again as a civilian."

"You probably will," she sighed. "And I'll be working in Woodward's Pharmacy in Brodie."

We heard the other car driving away, its automatic shift

performing in smooth and perfect order. The many great tires of a semi whined its approach from the other direction and roared past with a violent gust of wind. As the vehicular sounds faded, the grass and tree limbs settled, and the quiet was interrupted only by the busy river. The sky was a darkening blue canopy, pierced by the many stars. Melinda trembled with the chill——or a thought. I touched her hand there on the rock step and smiled to her. The air was damp and mysterious. Colors surrendered to the night. An animal cry echoed from a canyon wall and was answered in kind.

NINE

"WE REALLY appreciate your coming by." Mrs. Brandon was not the woman I had known as David's eternally cheerful mother. Her once expressive eyes now expressed only sadness. Her skin was drawn and pale. Her lips were smiling, but her face was grim. Whereas her husband sported a silver mane in the old hellfire and brimstone preacher fashion, her hair was now dull gray, combed into a matronly bun.

"I wanted to come sooner."

"We understand," Mrs. Brandon said. "You needed to spend a few days with your mother."

"Some things take a little time." Brother Brandon's gentle voice resonated throughout the room.

I cleared my throat and looked away. The darkness of the room made indistinguishable the color of its walls. Curtains drawn, sofa and chairs slick with wear, polished pieces of wood furniture old and sturdy. Everything belonged to the church. Mrs. Brandon's personal touches were few. In the hallway, David's college graduation portrait hung beside a portrait of his older sister and her family.

"Sometimes we don't understand God's ways," Brother Brandon continued. "But he has a purpose in all things." I now understood Brother Brandon's appeal to his congregation, his deep but tender voice a salve to wounded souls. He could implore and persuade the most reluctant heart to come forward and kneel before the pulpit.

"David was my best friend—"

"We know." From both.

I managed to compose myself under their glassy gaze. "We wrote to each other the whole time he was in the army."

"Yes," smiled Mrs. Brandon. "I'm sure he enjoyed that."

"I told him all about the islands I went to and the storms at sea and the dolphins and sharks." I knew that I was rambling, but I could not stop myself.

Brother Brandon nodded. "How well I remember twice crossing the sea during World War II."

His wife's smile broadened, but her eyes remained the same. "The sea must have been exciting."

"Yes," I said. "And so far removed from what's going on in the world."

"Far from the world but not from God."

"I wished David had signed up with me on the buddy system before the war was escalated."

"He really considered it," Mrs. Brandon said.

"I had no idea a war was coming. I only wanted to take some time off from college and see some of the world. I even came close to joining the army. Looking back now, everything seemed so simple then."

"Everything seems simple to a young man." Brother Brandon's deep voice beckoned like a distant horn in a fog.

"Even when David was called, I figured he'd be sent to Germany. And when I found out it would be Vietnam—. It didn't seem real."

"It was all like a dream," said Mrs. Brandon.

"It didn't become real until he wrote me from over there. He wrote about the people. And the dangers. Sometimes I envied him. I thought his adventures were greater than mine. He was taking part in something much more significant. But I was scared for him. I was glad I'd gotten in before I had to make the decisions he had to make."

"We couldn't know the war was coming," Mrs. Brandon said. "We all thought it best that he finish college. He wanted to teach school. Otherwise, he may have gone with you."

Her husband rested his great arms on his lap. "You can be

sure that God had a hand in helping you decide to leave college," he said. "You were an only child. Now that your mother is alone, she needs you. You were spared the decision because it wasn't yours to make."

How many only children have been killed in this war? I thought. *How many mothers have needed them?*

"We shouldn't question God's ways," Mrs. Brandon added kindly.

"I'm not questioning God," I answered. "I just wonder what the point of it all is. If I'd been forced to make a decision—to go or enlist—I wonder what I would have done. If I had it to make today, I wonder what I would do." I looked up to them and, for the first time, fully met their eyes. My dilemma had not reached them. Their answers were simple. They did not question. Everything was in God's hands. David's loss was a terrible blow, but they would endure. It was not up to them to find purpose in his death.

I wanted to throw open the curtains, to fill the room with light. I wanted to write across David's portrait, "He died that we might be free!" But I knew that wasn't true. He'd been killed by a mindless device set by a man who may never have learned that he had become a killer. David died only that someone else might take his place in battle.

Perhaps the Brandon's only challenge was to survive their son's death. That was my challenge, too, but I also wanted to understand. I wanted redemption not from my sins but from the irrational guilt I felt for not saving my friend.

"When tragedy takes our loved ones," Brother Brandon said, "our most difficult struggle is to maintain our faith. We must not lose our belief in God's mercy."

"I guess that's where my struggle is now," I answered.

"It's a struggle you must win."

Taking my leave, I reentered an outside world bright with mid-afternoon sunlight. My image of the Reverend and Mrs. Brandon was forever shattered. They would always be two wilting figures in a dark room, trusting in a greater design to give reason to their loss. But their eyes and hands belied the smiles. Their ghostly skin exposed dark habits.

Midday light stung my eyes. A boy pedaled his bike down the street, a clothespin-held square of cardboard clacking imitation motorcycle noises against the spokes. A kite burned red in the sky over the schoolhouse.

TEN

I AWOKE TO the glare of morning on the wall opposite my window. Roosters from the backyard pens of the few houses still clinging to tradition made their ritual announcement. I felt inexplicably refreshed. Maybe it was the contrast to the frantic shipboard reveilles not so far behind me. The 'I'm really home' thought still rolled across my taste buds. Shoving the quilts away, I stretched my limbs onto the invigorating coolness of the linoleum floor. For a moment I stood in the warm path of the sun, letting its energy unwind through my body. Before dressing and making the bed, I even performed a series of limbering up exercises I recalled from pre-Navy days.

Mother was still asleep when I entered the hall. A quick check of the hall clock told me that her ancient little alarm would sound in about fifteen minutes. The house lay invitingly still. But the floors squeaked thunderously with each step. Tiptoeing into the kitchen , I set breakfast in motion with a near catastrophic attempt to be quiet.

It was to be the first time in my life to cook breakfast for Mother. In the past, Daddy had cooked all the meals when Mother wasn't able. Daddy had spent World War II cooking for POWs somewhere near Boston. I wondered if he had known the same Boston I later discovered. We'd had so little time to talk about it. My one leave after my assignment to Boston as home port had been all too brief. And then the heart attack. And the emergency leave. And the funeral.

Daddy could crack and drop four eggs into the pan at the same time. But his cooking for Mother had had nothing to do with his army experiences. They were tender toward each other.

Daddy's coarse, strong hands could hold a rose against Mother's cheek and not crush it.

I heard Mother's first stirrings as I poured steaming water into the dripolator. It wasn't time for the alarm. She really tried to sleep a little later these days, but it was a rare morning when she didn't beat the alarm.

I had the table set when she came in.

"Well, what's going on in here?"

"Breakfast. I believe you want yours scrambled?"

"My, my." She sat at her place as I poured our coffee. "I don't know what to say. Except 'thank you.'"

"No thanks necessary." I sat down, watching Mother butter her toast."

"Are you going to eat or just watch me this morning?"

"Oh, I guess I was feeling a little proud of myself."

"You should. I couldn't have ordered it any better."

We ate more or less in silence, talking at times but not really saying anything. I'd never seen Mother more relaxed. All those Christmas and Thanksgiving dinners crossed my mind. Daddy and I had played minor roles, but Mother had always been the general. Her enjoyment had always seemed, at least to me, to be in the making rather than in the partaking of the meal. I could understand the battles being waged now against traditional roles of women, but I found them difficult to apply to my parents. Each had roles, to be sure, but they helped each other as best they could to perform their roles. Daddy did not come home at six o'clock and vegetate while Mother slaved in the kitchen. Daddy usually came home after dark, physically exhausted and covered with dust, washing up and sitting down to a late supper delayed for his arrival. At times, I would have been working after school with Daddy and would arrive with him. But usually I would not, so if there were blame for Mother's overwork in the kitchen, it was mine for not volunteering. As an only child, I often had been enlisted to help Mother with her household work. Volunteering to do even more of what was then considered women's work was not in the cards.

When we had finished, I was up and clearing the table before Mother had the chance. And then I refilled our cups and returned to my place.

"Your daddy would appreciate what you did."

I looked away, surprised. And then I felt Mother's hand on my arm. I turned back to meet her eyes. Her hand still reached across the table. The morning sparkled sadly in those eyes. With lips pressed tight and thin, with lines of years and sorrow, she spoke to me eloquently in a expression that said: it's time we talked about it.

We sat—I in my jeans and shirt, she in her long robe—surrounded by cookery, white enameled appliances, and all the growing-up years of my lifetime. We should have been three.

The trembling started way down in my lungs. It clasped my throat and spread cold and moist over my skin. My chest heaved and wet streams rolled down my face. I cradled my head into the shelter of my folded arms. My own sounds came from a great distance, from an abyss black and warm. I could feel Mother's pulse on my skin.

"I know," she said. And that was all there was to say.

When the trembling stopped, it stopped at once, the taste of salt still on my lips. My eyes burned softly. The awkward moment of reaching for my handkerchief. The harsh but necessary intrusion of blowing my nose.

"Crying can be a messy business," I said.

Mother smiled. "I'm sorry."

"I understand." I knew that Mother had wanted the moment to come when we were both strong. "Nighttime is no time to start crying," I had once heard her say.

"We were very lucky, you know—having your daddy all those years." Behind the sad lines, her face brightened as she spoke. "I guess I was luckier. I had him even longer."

"I never told him how proud of him I was."

"Yes, you did." Mother gripped my arm. "He was proud of his son, too. He may never have said it to you, but I know you felt it."

"Yes," I answered.

"It hasn't been easy. Your being so far away. Not knowing how you were taking it. Finding out how many ways we depended on him." The glow visually faded as she talked. And I felt at one with her in a way I'd never experienced. But she would not cry. I could see that.

"You were alone," I said.

"I had support—from church, from friends. You find out in those times how people really care."

"I worried so much for you."

She looked away a moment before speaking. For an instant I glimpsed the schoolteacher. So compassionate. So understanding. So much in control. "I know. And it would have been a comfort to have you here. Some things, though, you must accept in order to survive."

With all the resources I could muster, I managed to smile. "We'll do more than that."

She returned my smile and made my own easier. We listened to the promise of morning growing around us, and together we entered a new phase.

Mother stood, patting my arm, then picking up her cup and the coffee pot. "You finish your coffee and go on about your business. I'm taking over the kitchen."

My coffee was still warm, though it seemed that I'd been crying forever. Looking up at Mother, I sensed that she needed to be alone with her thoughts. I stood and gave her a brief hug, just long enough to hold the emotions at bay and then went quickly outside.

ELEVEN

THE SKY rumbled as rising swirls of dust danced across the fields. Enough spring rain remained to support the few mudhens floating close to the lake grass. Every step I took stirred clouds of mosquitoes. Terraces now circled the lake like a drawing on a topography map. Daddy had always said that terraces would be a waste of money. I still wondered if that had been only his mental defense against his inability to afford the expense. This day, though, the ominous spacing of the surviving young cotton plants testified to his wisdom. No more than an acre of water stood in the lake. Unless the clouds opened, the lake bed would soon be dry.

Above the first terrace I knelt and scooped a handful of soil. Below the crust the powdery dirt was hot even under a darkening sky. With bare hands, I dug nearly a foot down without finding moisture. A large whiteweed grew nearby. I grabbed it quickly, cheating the tiny thorns, and pulled it out. The first sign of moisture was more than a foot down the root.

Even at sea I'd never seen clouds that moved as those over the plains. The several layers were at odds with each other, one almost stationary, another a scattered patch of smoky blotches racing westward, and still another, the higher one, going south. Damp air, mosquito lotion, and sweat glued the loose clothing to my skin, and gusts of wet wind tossed my hair one way and then the other. From several directions, unmuffled irrigation engines challenged the threat of rain. They'd seen it before. They said they would see it again before the thirsty earth tasted water from above.

Standing now on the terrace, gazing around me, I saw not

Daddy's land but another man's work. The land had not the marks of Daddy's plow, nor the crops his character. I knew I would have to wait for another time to walk this ground and feel what I had expected to feel. The growing sadness I felt now was not for loss but for change, a change that left me breathless and made me want to move and not return until I had learned to accept it.

As I circled the edge of the lake toward my car, an old jackrabbit sprang from behind a clump of Johnson grass almost at my feet. The sudden rustling of the blades set my heart in rhythm with the rapid pounding of the rabbit's feet darting across the terraces, kicking up puffs of dust yards apart until he came to rest four terraces away, sitting immediately and sizing up the situation in profile.

Overhead, a pair of bullbats dipped and soared—a sure sign of rain, I'd often been told. Today I was not convinced. Over in Tayloe's pasture, cows huddled together. To the west, lightning split the horizon, followed seconds later by a dull crack that reminded me of a melon breaking open. "Just maybe," I whispered.

I jumped the bar'ditch and opened the car door. The interior was an oven. A dragonfly buzzed desperately against the windshield. Swatting it out, I sat half inside, half outside the car, waiting to catch my breath.

Driving toward Zack's, I switched the radio from station to station, searching for a weather report. The deejays, however, seemed oblivious to the weather. Lightning punctuated their songs with crashes of static, but the music played on. I switched off the radio and turned my attention to the clouds.

I could see that Zack had a good stand of cotton. The plants were closely spaced and uniformly tall, their dark leaves fluttering in the wind. The maize was taller and was growing well. It was like two good first cards at five card stud. Approaching the house, I saw Zack's red Farmall a quarter mile away pulling a rotary hoe.

The wind was picking up. I parked by Zack's truck and stood

in the yard, scanning the clouds. No areas of the green that always seemed to forewarn hail colored the sky, but a line of showers streaked from the clouds in the distance. I'd seen many little tornadoes playing at the bottoms of similar clouds far above the ground, but none appeared today.

Spider met me at the back door, stretching as he rose. He ambled stiff-legged to me until he was within reach and stood motionless as I petted him. I went through the kitchen to Zack's version of a living room and found the telephone. Mother would be aware of the clouds. I caught her at home and told her where I was and not to be surprised if rain and muddy roads kept me overnight.

Windows rattled slightly with each gust that swished through the trees outside. I went from room to room, checking for open windows.

Zack's house was arranged in the practical manner of one who never expects company. The three or four rooms contained nothing decorative except a few wildlife scenes he'd clipped from *Texas Parks and Wildlife*, the pictures tacked at odd places in each room. The fourth room was a small bedroom Zack used as a combination open closet and bathroom. An iron pipe supported in the center and reaching across the length of the room was more than ample space for the dozen or so sets of shirts and pants that hung neatly against the outer wall. A dark blue, pleated and narrow-lapelled suit hung off to one side. Zack owned one raincoat, one light denim jacket, and one heavy war surplus jacket. The only bathroom fixture was an elongated galvanized tub that he had attached to the floor and provided with a drain. Bath water, though, still had to be carried from the kitchen.

The bedroom was stark: an unpolished wood floor, an iron bed, a square, sturdy dresser. The living room floor was covered with the same linoleum as in the kitchen. An early-model television set was in one corner by the seldom-used front door, with a recliner and two other chairs facing it. By the recliner was a smoke stand, a stack of paperback western novels, and a pint of the whiskey that Zack sometimes mixed with his coffee.

Over the TV, in cardboard folders, were several photographs of Zack's son Mark at various ages. I vaguely remembered Zack's wife. She had long since taken her infant son to California, leaving her husband to his odd little house and his dusty dreams. For twenty years Zack had sent money and gifts and had made the trek to the coast for a week or two in the winter. He never talked of his son, and I never asked. One summer, in the driest of years, a skinny twelve-year-old kid wearing Bermuda shorts and sneakers had spent a month with his dad. All summer that year the wind swept down from the Colorado Rockies, gaining momentum down the Texas Panhandle and blowing great clouds of dust in magnificent fashion over the plains. Zack was constantly in the fields, crisscrossing the young crops and vulnerable topsoil with his tractor and sandfighter and staying up all hours of the night, tending the irrigation water. The kid hated the flat land, the wind, the dust, the cows, the outdoor toilet. He found no games to play around the farm buildings three miles from town. He told me in a peculiar accent of palm trees and freeways. He called West Texas a desert and vowed never to return.

I went back to the kitchen and took a coke from the refrigerator. Spider lay on the floor by the table. He lifted and dropped his tail once as I passed on my way to the back door.

The sky had grown much darker, with shower lines visible in several directions. Wind blew wet and cool through my hair. To the west, sunlight streaked bright yellow through a hole in the clouds. Blowing dust marked the dirt roads between the fields. A well motor suddenly died away, and I realized that all the area wells had been silenced.

Zack had unhitched the rotary hoe and was coming down the turn row. Going back into the house, I opened another coke. Zack had the tractor under the shed and was walking toward the house when I stepped back outside. I met him by the windmill tower, and he downed half the coke before speaking.

"Whatcha think?" he asked. His clothes and skin were

coated light brown. Large wet spots showed under his arms and across his back.

"Looks like it might do it."

He took off his cap and slapped it against his leg, the cap's dust claimed quickly by the wind. "Might," he said.

We finished our cokes silently, surveying the storm's progress. I shivered against the wind. The temperature was down at least twenty degrees since noon. An occasional moment of stillness would come and then the wind would rush in from another direction.

Zack tossed the empty into the weeds by the cowshed. Mine followed. "Heard any reports?" he asked.

"Not much."

"We'll go turn on the radio."

Following Zack to the house, I took a last look around. Cattle were coming in from the pasture, single file with heads bent low to the ground. A family of quail rushed across their path to their shelter in the weeds around the parked implements. The first few heavy drops of rain scattered over the ground.

We hurried to the porch, and Zack latched the screen door behind us as Spider watched anxiously from the kitchen. After moving the few vulnerable items inside, we returned to the porch. Zack's was the only screened-in porch I knew of on the plains. It was totally impractical, but he didn't seem to mind occasionally moving everything inside to hose it down after a spring dust storm. I'd always figured the porch had been built to please his wife.

Wet spots polka dotted the ground, but the dry spaces quickly filled in. Zack tapped my shoulder and pointed out past the windmill tower. A wall of water rapidly neared. The sky had become almost black. For a moment the whole earth was still. Tree limbs, the cows in the lot, clumps of carelessweeds growing against the toolshed were like a photograph.

It hit with startling suddenness. Raindrops pounded the porch roof like the roll of a thousand snare drums. The yard was an instant lake. Within seconds I lost sight of the windmill tower.

"Think it might rain," Zack said with a pure deadpan expression.

"I'd say a twenty percent chance."

Just as suddenly as the rain hit, the wind returned, spraying the porch with water. We rushed into the house.

Zack handed me a paper towel, and I wiped the dampness from my face and arms and then sat on the floor by Spider, giving him a good rubdown. Spider half-climbed into my lap, resting his chin over his paws. Zack went immediately to making coffee. While the coffee perked, he removed his outer clothes and washed himself at the sink. We turned on the radio but soon got tired of the static. The brief weather report mentioned only scattered thunderstorms.

"Better figure on stayin' over."

"Might have to." Spider was asleep on my lap, snoring like an exhausted child, his breath warm on my leg. I eased myself free without waking him and went to the window. "We won't even notice when the sun goes down," I said.

"Not unless the rain stops first." He turned off the burner under the percolator. "Sure could use come *easy* rain."

After pouring us each a cup, he went out of the room, returning with the whiskey bottle and a fresh set of clothes. "Thought you might want to add a little flavor," he said. I pushed my cup over. He measured it out with a tablespoon and stirred it into each cup. He washed at the sink and after he'd put on his clean clothes, we sat at the table, sipping our coffee, listening to the rain.

"You know, this farmin's gettin' a damn sight harder ever' year," Zack said. "Thirty years ago the price of cotton was twenty-five cents a pound and a good four-row tractor and equipment was goin' for three thousand. Today it's still twenty-five cents, and a tractor *without* implements'll set you back seventeen thousand. And the way things are goin', it'll be *thirty* in another ten years."

"Cost of livin'," I said.

"Cost of livin', hell! It's them union workers makin' nine

dollars an hour up North. You can't get nobody to do farm work for what you can pay'em. Government wants us to pay a dollar sixty an hour. Hell, I ain't makin' a dollar sixty!"

"You got me there," I answered. "Still, I see the government's point. It's awful hard for anybody to live these days even at that wage."

Zack took a long sip from his saucer. "Yeah," he said, "you can't blame a man wantin' to make a decent livin' for his family. You take these Mex'cans. They're good family people. They might raise a little hell on Saturday night, but they try to take care of their kids. And, hell, you'll see a whole family out in the field tryin' to make enough to get by."

The inequity of farm labor wages was one of the more complicated questions I'd struggled with while on the farm and in my years away. The lifestyles forced on those people had always struck me as a disgrace. And yet I knew also that higher wages would mean the end of small farms like Daddy's and Zack's. "How do you manage without help?" I asked.

"Herbicides. Costs like hell, too. Course, ever' now and then I have to have a little extra help."

"Maybe I could help you some." Zack lifted his saucer, eyeing me through the steam. "Just when you need me this summer. Until school starts."

He put the saucer down and cocked his ear to the rain. "Oh, I don't know. Couldn't pay you no more'n I could anybody else."

"Not talkin' about pay. I need some exercise."

"Don't know. I reckon I can get along." He stood and walked toward the refrigerator. "You still play dominoes?"

"It's been awhile. Yankees don't know what their for."

"Yankees don't know a lot of things. Let's eat some supper and see if you can beat me."

While I brewed a pitcher of iced tea, Zack reheated a pot of red beans and salt pork and a pan of fried okra.

The window was black when I looked up after supper. All through the meal, the storm had alternated between driving rain and gentle showers. On the floor, Spider snored softly through it all. But the slightest shift of wind or change in the patter of rain reflected on Zack's mobile face. A hard rain would pelt the leaves and stems of the growing crops, leaving the ground hard, the crust barely penetrated, and valuable topsoil washed away. Too much standing water could cause root rot.

At dominoes Zack played to win, never missing a shot. Every domino he played added up to fives and every time I thought I had him blocked, he had the right numbers in the hole. Every domino placed on the table registered automatically in Zack's mind. Had I tried to keep tabs as well, the game would have ground to a halt. I managed one win out of five games, and that came when the rainfall was especially fierce, stealing Zack's attention from the game. Staying up late was of no concern. There would be no work done in the fields tomorrow.

We played until the rain stopped. It died slowly, winding down in the hours toward midnight. Zack poured out the coffee dregs and rinsed the pot. Spider yawned, raising his head momentarily to the noise, then stretched out again and went back to sleep.

In the bedroom, Zack opened a window, and the damp chill crept in, unusually cool for the season. We stripped to our shorts and got into bed. Zack rolled to one side and was asleep in minutes, his breathing surprisingly light.

I closed my eyes and tried to remember the sound of the rain. Somehow, I found myself at the wheel of Daddy's old two-cylinder poppin' Johnny tractor. It was going backward, and I turned to look behind just as the back wheels rolled over the edge of the cliff.

I felt the bed jerk as I awoke. Zack remained asleep. I lay back and tried to stay awake until my muscles relaxed, hoping that the next time I would fall into restful sleep at once. I thought of the night's storm and was reminded of the storm off Cape Hatteras in the winter of '65 and how the wave caps, they said, had reached seventy feet. The several smaller escorts had turned into the waves and made their way back to port. But the great carrier, taking several waves at once, had been at the mercy of the angry storm, toppling and bobbing like a cork in a fish pond.

Furious waves twisted and tore away the catwalks and forward antennas. With the crest of a giant swell at midship, the bow dipped frighteningly low, with no time to recover before the next onslaught surged over the forward flight deck, rushing a mass of churning white foam against the superstructure. The bow rose to the top of the next wave, throwing sheets of water hundreds of feet into the air. And when the bow crashed back to the sea, the spray shot from both sides far across the waters. The fore and aft sections would rise and fall a hundred feet with each wave. For ten days it lasted. The world pitched and rolled and turned, giving no indication that it would ever return to normal. Everything was tied down. Chairs were lashed to bulkheads. Meals were served without drinks. I could see objects falling to the decks, a life raft floating down the hangar deck, Zack's tractor smashing into a secured helicopter. It went on. Until finally the waves settled. The wind blew crisply over the ocean. Starlight danced on the wave caps. The full moon appeared boastfully before darting behind a cloud.

TWELVE

I AWOKE TO the aroma of fresh-brewed coffee. The clock by the bed said eight-thirty. By the time I'd dressed and got to the kitchen, Zack had bacon on two plates and eggs frying in the skillet.

"Thought you were gonna sleep all day."

I looked past him out the kitchen door and saw tracks across the yard. "If I hadn't smelled that coffee, I'd of been there 'til noon."

Zack chuckled. "Does kinda wake a fella up."

"How much you get."

"Bit over two inches. First inch came hard, though. I don't think it did much good 'cept to beat the ground down. Took a lotta leaves."

I went to the back porch and looked over the yard. Spider stood and came to me, wagging his tail. His hair was soft and wet to the touch and smelled of damp green weeds. He looked five years younger.

"Kinda muddy out," said Zack. "Got any boots?"

"Never thought of it."

"I got an old pair. We'll take a walk after breakfast."

I couldn't remember ever having started the morning with a tastier meal. With the eggs and bacon, we had pan toast dripping with honey and sorghum molasses, and we washed it all down with very black coffee. Standard fare for Zack. I lingered over the third cup while Zack rummaged through a box of old shoes and boots, finally coming out with a pair of rubber ones that had once been his boots for irrigating.

I washed the dishes while Zack fed Spider on the back porch

from a box of meat scraps Sonny had given him. Spider looked up at Zack and moaned anxiously until his pan was full, all the while his tail going from side to side in appreciation.

With breakfast over and Spider fed, we went outside to survey the effect of the rain. Our footprints sank two inches into the mud, the loose boots trying to come of my feet with each step; apparently, the ground did get some soaking. The sky spanned even bluer than the first day I'd arrived back. Everything had a fresh-washed look. In the pasture, the faces of the cows shone remarkably white under the mid-morning sun. Under the cattle's feet, short buffalo grass still held the pasture soil firm. In the yard, the bare ground was dark with moisture. Every low spot was a pond. Down the turn row, the runoff had created miniature valleys and canyons.

"What do you think?" I asked.

"Don't know. Mighta done me some good."

We walked on. From underneath a harrow, two cottontails rushed through the grass and weeds to an old cotton stripper. As we neared the low spot in the pasture, a cacophony of frogs overwhelmed all other sounds. With long-jointed twigs for legs, a blue heron pranced across the water, its head darting from side to side, occasionally scooping into the water. Two white birds I didn't recognize flew low over the heron, circling the lake and landing on the other side.

"Cowbirds," Zack said. "Some call'em 'ee—grets'. They're comin' up from Mexico and takin' over the country."

Zack's maize showed a little more effect from the downpour. Almost every plant had a leaf or two pounded into the mud, but the bulk of the leaves were erect and undamaged.

"Goin' fishin'?" I asked. Zack and Daddy used to do a lot of fishing together when it was too wet to plow. During growing season, that was about the only chance they had for a break, and, if the rain or hail was particularly destructive, fishing was a good way to get their minds off the damage.

"Nope," Zack answered. "Haven't been lately."

He leaned against a fence post by the turn row. Something

splashed in the pasture lake, and, for a brief while, the frogs were silent.

"Got a lot of things to do," Zack said.

"I'll help you."

Zack looked back to the house. "No need."

I could have said that I wanted to work for my supper, but that would have been insulting. "For my stiff joints," I said. "They need greasing."

Zack bent down and pulled up a young devil's claw. He looked back toward the house, needing a little time to settle things in his mind. Zack had given a lot of his neighbors, his time and labor when they needed it, but giving was a lot easier than receiving. "Gotta fix a flat on the cultivator," he finally said. "Ditcher needs a little weldin'."

"Let's get started."

Zack turned back to me. "I'd never ask—"

"Hell, man," I said, starting back to the house. "I'm the one that's askin'."

The rest of the day was just plain hard work. Repairing the flat was not much of a problem, but Zack had to tell me where anything I needed was stored. His filing system was simple; he just remembered the last place he had used each item and laid it down. We decided against welding the ditcher because we couldn't figure a way to keep our feet off the wet ground.

The next job was the toughest and was, in fact, one of my least favorite when helping Daddy. Zack had spotted pink eye on two of his cows, meaning that those had to be doctored and the others inspected. After putting down a layer of dry hay, we fed the herd up into the lot, except for a few stragglers that had to be driven. One ornery little heifer broke and managed to slip between two loose strands of barbed wire, stepping on and stretching the wire in the process, eliciting a few choice words from Zack's direction before we got her back with the others. And then it was a matter of isolating each animal, dodging hooves, enduring ropeburn and manure. Then it was a matter of examining fast, doctoring when necessary, and getting the ropes off without getting maimed.

As we left the cow lot, Zack pulled a four-foot-tall careless-weed, mostly just to remove it from his path, and then we more or less fell into the job of pulling a forest of the enormous weeds that bordered the lot and surrounded some of the other outbuildings. Zack had been turning up tiny new carelessweeds by the millions with his rotary hoe just before the rain hit. These we pulled now had reached their present size only because Zack's workload had left this job on the back burner. Compared to the last job, this one was almost fun; it was so easy pulling the weeds up from the loose mud, knowing that they would be hell to hoe in dry weather.

Mosquitoes waged a constant battle against us. Giving up on insect lotion, we built a fire with some of the chicken house lumber and threw the pulled green weeds on top, making the air thick with smoke. Then we stood in the midst of it, turning until our skin and clothing had been completely exposed. Zack said that it was the method the Indians had used. I didn't know, but it seemed to help.

To aid our getting around, we laid planks across the softer mud and standing water. Occasionally, I checked the condition of the road leading toward town, but this fertile earth held moisture well, and the sun, though unhampered by clouds, appeared to have had little drying effect. Instead, the air stayed cool. I felt hot with heavy work even with all the sweat, but now and then a cool breeze quickly reminded me of the lower temperature.

Toward late afternoon, I realized that the roads would not improve. Zack offered to pull my car to the main road with his tractor, but there was no use putting deep ruts in his turn row, so I borrowed his denim jacket and rubber boots, said goodbye to Spider, and made my way toward home.

The county road was hard mud the last mile or so to town, as though the rain had been heavier here but brief. In spots, tiny insect trails crisscrossed each other. The odd trail of a reptile went perpendicular across the road with finely detailed footprints on each side of a sliding trench. The last remaining traces of tire ruts from a former rain had been rounded off, making the roadbed almost as smooth as fresh asphalt. In places, though, the surface was as soft as the plowed fields, and I doubted that I would have made it through by car.

A half-mile from town, deep automobile tracks began abruptly in the ditch and doubled snake-fashion back to town. Deeply imprinted over the meandering smaller tracks were the deliberate, straight tracks of the tractor that had pulled the car out. I walked in the tractor ruts until they turned off at the last farm house outside town. Beyond that was the pavement.

Walking into town was entering another world. I'd always sensed that even small town folks were far removed in spirit from the farmers. My first memories were of a house as small and utilitarian as Zack's. When Mother had taken the high school English position and two years later we'd moved to town, I still considered myself farm folk.

Beneath the elms, the air was as crisp as early winter. I fastened the top button of Zack's jacket and pulled my arms in tight. The western sky was smeared purple and orange. Not a pretty sunset at all by South Plains standards. Everywhere, muddy tracks streaked the pavement. Pickups were caked with dark-brown mud. In a circular rainwater puddle around a rosebush, a toy battleship lay on its side.

THIRTEEN

T HE DAY was August 22, 1962, the first of the two days I
remember most when I think of my father. What was
remarkable about that day was that it was in the middle
of the week, the sky was clear, maize stalks had yet to be plowed
under, we'd been waiting for a day to take some steers to
market——and Daddy asked me if I'd like to go fishing.

I had not been fishing with my father in almost two years,
and he had not asked me to go in about one year. Over time, I
had simply lost interest, "fished myself out," I'd tell people. The
preparation, the discomfort, the smell, the fact that I did not
particularly care for the taste of fish and especially did not care
to clean them——all had led to my dwindling enthusiasm. During
those two years, telling Daddy no and, later, watching him make
his preparations without asking if I'd like to join him had
weighed on my conscience. I was in my late teens, moving away
from my parents and their world and toward my friends and the
world that we imagined awaited us. So, why on this late August
day in 1962 did my father decide to go fishing——and ask me to
join? I knew why. In the eighteen years of my life, my father had
been alone with me in two ways, working in the fields and
fishing. Daddy wanted to spend time alone with me in my last
week before leaving home for college and this way was the only
way he knew how.

"Should I pack enough food to last all night?"

"It's up to you," Daddy answered. "We can come home
tonight if you want."

Daddy seldom went fishing for only a few hours. Almost
always, he would fish all night, and, often, he would come home,

drink a quick cup of coffee, and hit the fields. Mother had worried for thirty years that he would go to sleep on his tractor, but he never did. I knew that Daddy paid too much attention to his work to drift into sleep. I also knew that he wanted to spend the night fishing. I packed sandwich meat, bread, and cinnamon rolls for the duration.

I listened to the familiar conversation between my mother and father:

"Do you want some of these oatmeal cookies packed in with your lunches?"

"Put a few in. Do we have some rye bread?"

Daddy was disorganized about some things but not about getting his fishing gear together. His rods and reels, tackle boxes, minnow buckets—the works—were all together in a corner of the garage. Mother would usually pull her car out of the drive, Daddy would back up to the garage, and in forty seconds it was done.

The truck was packed and the engine running before I'd changed into my fishing clothes. Daddy called from the back door but with noticeably less urgency than I remembered from earlier trips.

"Be there in a minute," I answered.

"Take your time. I got your rubber boots."

"Thanks."

Getting ready for fishing was not like getting ready to plow. There were certain clothes you wore, clothes that had a lingering smell of fish, clothes that you would not wear anywhere else. Most of those clothes, except for my old fishing cap, I'd outgrown since my last trip. I had to find my least-valued shirt and jeans.

"Be sure you put on plenty of mosquito lotion," Mother advised when I emerged from my room. "You know how they ate you up the last time." That, I remembered, was another reason I'd lost interest.

"I won't forget," I answered.

Mother gave us each a kiss and a hug. Mine were brief but loving. Daddy's would have been memorable, had it not been that their goodbyes were always so warm. In earlier years, those displays had embarrassed me. Now, they reassured me.

We were off. Through town, Daddy nodded or gave the two-fingers off the steering wheel Texas salute to everyone we saw——on foot or in other vehicles. I wondered if they saw our fishing gear and thought us lazy to be idling away a good work day. Daddy, I'm sure, never gave it a thought.

Out of town, we were on the four-lane divided highway, headed in the same direction Melinda and I would travel six years later. Daddy noticed every crop and commented on particularly abundant ones. He admired them; I envied their owners. Had Daddy had their big tractors, their irrigation wells, their level vast fields, I knew that his would have matched them easily.

"You won't see crops like this in the country where you're headed." It was Daddy's way of bringing up the subject of my leaving.

"No, I guess not." Casual conversation with my father had always been a little strained. When we worked together, it was no problem. Casual exchanges could be interjected between the normal talk of work. Otherwise, we needed a subject to talk about before the words came easily. But it had never been the words that mattered.

"East Texas cotton, though, is all open by now. Might be stripping it before you get there."

"Could be," I said. "Looked nearly ready my last trip out."

Daddy had surprised me when we did not turn toward Buffalo Lakes. I knew that we were headed to Lake Stamford. It was a much longer trip. We'd have only an hour or so of daylight when we arrived.

My ears stopped up as soon as we dropped off the caprock. I could feel, more than hear, the rumble of the engine and Daddy's infrequent talk. Finally, with lots of hard swallows, my ears cleared. The engine roared and the wind whistled like a January blizzard past the window. Occasionally we saw sparse dryland cotton struggling in the harsh condition below the caprock. These farmers, I thought, would give their right arms to have Daddy's land.

In the canyon we turned south toward Spur. This was cattle country. This land had the appearance that the moviegoer assumed was all of Texas. Around stock tanks and creek beds bush mesquites had grown into shade trees. Prickly pear cactus climbed up through barbed wire fences.

"You got everything you need for college?" Daddy did not lead into a subject.

"As far as I know."

"Well, you may find out when you get there you overlooked something. Just let us know."

"I will," I answered. "I can't imagine what it would be, though."

We arrived at the lake late in the afternoon. Within minutes, it seemed, the lines were cast and the rods stood erect in their holders. Daddy fished only for catfish. There was no need for a camp; we would not sleep or cook. The coffee was in thermoses and the sandwiches packed in ice. All we took out, besides the fishing gear, were a couple of old folding chairs and the Coleman lantern.

We covered ourselves with mosquito lotion and settled in for what I anticipated as long hours of idleness. Daddy could stare at his lines for hours, sensitive to any twitch or bend in the rods. I wished I'd brought a book.

"I remember when your mother was at college," Daddy said. We had been sitting quietly for fifteen minutes. I turned to face him. Unlike some men of few words I knew, Daddy always looked his subject in the eyes and always with a comfortable grin.

"It must have been a tough time for you. I barely remember any of it."

"It was—a little. She had to sit out a semester when you were born."

"She really must have had it rough," I said. "All those years going part time."

"She knew what she wanted." In that moment, I saw the pride in Daddy's eyes, and a question I'd harbored for years was answered. Daddy felt no resentment that Mother was more educated than he or that her employment provided us with more financial security. Daddy was all man—in every way, but to him masculinity had nothing to do with superiority.

"Are you gonna be all right?" I asked. "I mean without me around to help on the farm?"

Daddy's grin widened. "You thought you were help?" he said.

"You mean I was just in the way?"

"No," he answered. "You were always a big help." He turned to check his lines and then turned back. "But I'll be okay."

"I'll be back summers." This was before my decision for summer classes.

"No," Daddy said. "I guess you'll have things to do. You've got your own life now."

I suddenly felt free in a way that I did not feel prepared to be. Daddy was not cutting me loose; he was recognizing my adulthood. This was my rite of passage. Momentarily I looked down, gathering my thoughts, and when I looked up, our eyes met briefly in an exchange I would always remember. And then we were both sitting back in our chairs, staring at the ripples crossing the point of entry of our lines.

When the sun set, we'd caught nothing. Daddy went to the pickup and brought back a sandwich for each of us. The first evening breeze crossed the water, and we poured our first coffee.

"Nothin's biting but the mosquitoes," I said.

"Maybe they'll start after dark."

An hour later, I was getting impatient, not at the slow passage of time, but at the lack of fishing success. It was the first time in several trips that I had really cared about catching a fish. Daddy's lines got a couple of nibbles, but mine remained as taut as when I'd first cast them out. I resisted the temptation to reel them in and check the bait. Another hour and I knew that I had to have a little sleep. I headed for the pickup.

"That's just more fish for me," Daddy called.

I awoke hurting everywhere. One knee was jammed against

the dashboard; the other, twisted under the steering wheel. Mosquitoes I'd been dreaming about turned out to be real. I massaged my neck and shoulders and pulled myself up into position to exit the cab.

Daddy turned up the lantern for a moment while he poured me some coffee. He reached over toward the waterline and pulled out his stringer with two just-large-enough channel catfish.

"Did you string those just to show me?" I asked, laughing.

"Thought they might be a record. Any smaller and they couldn't get the hook in their mouths."

I rubbed my eyes. The smell of bait and lake water was on my hands. My body still ached and itched and my ears were bombarded by the racket of frogs and insects. But it didn't matter. For the first time in years, it didn't matter. I wanted to spend this time with my father. Perhaps, when I was very young, Daddy had taken me somewhere just to be with me. Perhaps he had done that many times as I grew older, without my knowing the reason. Before my teens, I had tagged along on numerous occasions just to be close. But this was the first time in my life that I knew the two of us were together because the two of us wanted to be.

I sipped the hot coffee and then set the cup aside to check my lines. Daddy lit a cigarette, the yellow glow accenting the wrinkles that I'd only recently begun to notice. I knew that I had been born later to my parents than were some of my friends, but reminders were always just a little painful. This time, it only made me feel closer.

"Did you ever think about going to college?" I asked.

Daddy took a long drag and slowly let the smoke go. "Not for long," he answered. "I thought about it a little after the war—on the G.I. Bill. Maybe if I'd been a little younger."

"Lots of people go when they're older. What about Mother?"

"Yeah, but she had her goal. She wanted to be a teacher."

I really knew why Daddy had not gone. His only interest was in farming, and, like most farmers of his era, he did not trust college ideas about agriculture. My reasons for entering college had little to do with a future career, though I knew that somewhere along the line I had to think about that. To most people, especially of my parents' generation, one attended college specifically to gain entry into a profession.

Daddy got himself an oatmeal cookie and pushed the sack over to me. "I bet you're gonna be gettin' boxes of these pretty soon," he said. "Your mother will probably forget all about cookin' for me."

I laughed. "Not a chance."

The hours passed, and the two of us continued talking about nothing special, at ease with each other as never before. Fish continued to ignore our lines. Twice we changed bait, hoping to find something that might appeal to them on that hot summer night. Even Daddy's special stink bait doused in whiskey could not get us a bite.

As the sky and the water turned orange with the first light of morning, I began to lose hope. The thermos coffee and all the food were gone. Minnows quickly took the last cookie crumbs as soon as I tossed them into the water. At least something was alive out there, I thought. Daddy got out his beat-up and blackened old coffee pot and dipped water directly from the lake. Before long, we had fresh boiled coffee.

"You about ready to give this up?" Daddy asked.

"Not really," I answered, gazing at my lines, hoping for at least one good bite before giving up. "I guess you really need to get on home, though, don't you."

We finished our coffee and pulled in the lines, discarding the bait. Ten minutes later, we were on our way. Dirty, a bit smelly, and looking as though we'd been up all night, we stopped in Stamford for breakfast. The locals, being so close to the lake, I hoped would be used to stinkers such as we. Back on the road, I offered a turn at the wheel, but Daddy declined. Gratefully, I surrendered to sleep, putting infinite trust in Daddy's ability to stay awake and get us safely home.

FOURTEEN

"D O I SEEM different to you?"

"Yes," Mother answered. "Because you *are* different. I'd have been foolish to have expected you not to change."

"But I feel sometimes that I've changed more than you would have wanted. More than even I would have wanted."

Mother folded the last washcloth and put it in the basket ready to be carried to the linen closet. I sat across the table, peeling potatoes for dinner—twelve noon Southern dinner. "I suppose there *are* some ways I wouldn't like to think you've changed. Certain values I hope you've held onto. I hope you haven't lost your faith in God."

I listened to the dry, restless wind outside—felt the stuffy heat. The soil had crusted over since last week's rain, and the west windows were closed against the resulting dusty air. "I guess some of my values have changed," I said. "It seems like the whole world has changed since the year I joined the Navy."

"The world is always changing. That's why it's important to guard your values."

"Maybe," I conceded.

Mother reached over the table and placed her hand on my arm. "You've had terrible things happen to you in losing David and then your daddy's dying so suddenly. But those things had nothing to do with your basic beliefs." She patted my arm, then took the pan of peeled potatoes and began slicing them.

"I really don't know," I said. "So many things have happened just this year. Assassinations, cities burning, riots." In the second week after my arrival home, Robert Kennedy had been assassinated. Two months before, it had been Martin Luther King. The nation seemed to be going mad. When I'd walked the streets of Brodie the day after the announcement of Kennedy's death, I heard no voice except Sonny's mention his name. "It's a damn shame," he had said. "I didn't agree with his politics, but no man would wish that much suffering on a family." A local pastor had declared the event to be evidence of God's displeasure with our growing permissiveness. I'd walked the streets alone, thinking of Homer's ancient Greeks, who had courted their chosen heroes, heroes who had failed them, through their inevitable flaws, by the unforgivable act of dying. "It's not a time for heroes," I'd whispered. Perhaps there had been too many heroes.

I looked across at Mother, who seemed to me to have been isolated from the happenings of the last few years. And I began to wonder what had been the the effect of happenings in other years. She had lived through a depression, buried both her parents, lost many friends in a bigger war, endured Daddy's battles with an unyielding farm. "Why," I had once asked Daddy, "did your Dad buy *this* farm?" His answer had been simple, accepting, reflecting none of my unconcealed frustration. "Because when he bought it, all the land around here was dryland and cotton prices were high. He considered himself lucky to find any land at all. And before irrigation it was just as good as any other place." He had chosen to farm his inherited land and had never looked back on his decision. And, as far as I knew, neither had my mother.

"I know it's little consolation," Mother said, "but a lot of people have suffered losses in the last few years." She surprised me by almost laughing. "Old Mrs. Murphy still keeps patting my arm and telling me, 'Sister Simpson, you just have to bear up under the load. Sometimes it's all I can do to keep from giggling." She went back to work on the potatoes. "She is a sweet old lady, and I know she wants to comfort me."

"I know what you mean," I said. "Guys on the ship treated me so different after Daddy died. They were afraid to laugh or talk loud or anything. It made me feel guilty."

"It meant they cared."

"I know. Even when David was killed, they wouldn't leave me alone. It was like everybody wanted a share of my pain." I stared down at the pile of potato peelings, profoundly aware of how mundane was my life considering the times. "I know they didn't realize what they were doing, but there we were, in the military, all the talk about Vietnam. And I was the only one who had actually lost somebody there. We were just playing war games against the Russians, while the real war was somewhere else. It was weird, but it was like they wanted some way to be a part of it."

Moments passed before Mother responded. "I don't know what to say to that," she said. "That's something I don't understand." She met my eyes when I looked up. "Give it a little time," she said. Maybe it's just that too much has happened at once."

"I hope you're right," I answered. But I knew she was not. Inside, I really knew she was wrong. If the world had changed, my perception had unalterably changed. And how could I expect Mother to understand the questions that had churned my guts, denied my sleep, eaten away at my long-conditioned reasonings? My mother—Mother who loved so deeply, who shared so openly her own joy and others' sorrow, who talked with Wordsworth at Tintern Abbey, who had made of herself what she wanted to be: wife, mother, servant of God, teacher—Mother who sometimes still called black people 'coloreds,' who did not question War. I loved her more profoundly than anyone alive.

After the meal, I helped her in the vegetable garden. To protect the plants against insects, we set out marigolds at intervals among the squash, cantaloupe, and crowder peas, following a theory she had recently read about in the paper. I had my doubts, but she wanted to give it a try. On an outside row, the okra was now six inches tall. In all my years of helping tend the garden, I'd developed practically no gardening skills; I'd always watered the rows Mother said needed water, spaced the plants as instructed. Every year I'd asked: How long until the okra will be ready? This year I would watch and wait.

"Aren't you going out to the farm today?" Mother asked.

"I don't think so. I'm afraid Zack's starting to feel pretty bad about my working without being paid."

"I've wondered about that."

"He doesn't say anything. But it shows."

"Maybe you ought to think about getting a job somewhere until fall. You never know what expenses you might run into in school." She stopped her weeding a moment and looked over to me. "You *are* still planning to go to school, aren't you?"

"I suppose."

"You don't sound very sure."

"Just bein' lazy, I guess. I'm seriously considering becoming a bum."

Mother laughed. "They may have to buy some new benches for downtown. We're getting more bums around here than we can handle."

I moved the water hose over to the new row Mother had just weeded. "I don't think I'd fit very well with Smiley's crowd."

"Don't tell me you're going to become a hippie." I noticed that trace of uncertainty that I'd caught at other times since coming home. That uncertainty that said: Yes, you *have* changed.

"I don't think I'd fit very well with that crowd either."

"I hope not. Your second cousin Frances has been giving her parents fits. She never seems to have an address where they can reach her. They say they don't even know her anymore, she's so different"

"Well, I don't know her at all. She's just a name I've heard."

Mother smiled. "I can't really see you with long hair and beads."

"You never know," I teased. "My Navy haircut hasn't had time to grow out yet. I might just let it grow down to my toes."

"We finished watering and weeding the last row, and we carried the garden tools back to the garage. While we'd been in the garden, the wind had almost died away, but inside the garage we could hear it whistling in above the door. The air smelled of dust, and the bottles along the wall had gathered a light brown film. Even yet, it seemed odd to me seeing objects resting quietly on the edge of a shelf, not subject to being tossed to the decks by the next ocean wave.

"Have you decided for sure where you're going to school?"

"Actually, I haven't decided for sure that I *am* going."

"Oh? You've been reading catalogs very closely."

"Well, I'm reasonably sure. I've got a couple of applications ready for mailing. Would you be very disappointed if I didn't go– –or maybe just waited a year or so?"

"Why, Alan! I'm surprised that you'd even ask."

I was surprised that she'd been hurt by my asking, but I immediately understood why.

"I didn't mean it that way."

"I don't have plans for you. Surely you weren't going to seek my approval before you made a decision."

"No. I really didn't mean it that way at all. I just know that I haven't been very definite about anything since I've been home. I guess the thing that seemed most definite was that I'd go to school."

Mother smiled again but this time with eyes that looked into a different time. "You'll make the right decision," she said. "That's the only thing I feel definite about." And then her eyes came back to me, to the present, to the whistling wind. "I guess I'll be dusting this place out tomorrow."

I said nothing. We put the garden tools in place. The bottles and jars seemed quite at home on their stable platforms.

Melinda called that evening. Why hadn't I been by to see her? "Perhaps tomorrow," I said. We talked until midnight.

FIFTEEN

WITHIN DAYS after the rain, the wind turned dry. I walked between cotton rows, hoe in hand, tasting sandy dust. Bending over at my work, I felt the sun hot on my neck above the raised collar. Under my shoes, freshly turned soil was moist, and I longed to feel its wetness on the soles of my feet. But I knew the sun would burn my ankles in minutes. Several hundred yards to my left, Zack, with his tractor and cultivator, appeared to be almost finished in the cotton land and would probably be into the maize by early afternoon. Other tractors in other fields were doing like work, giving me hope that the blowing dust would soon be confined to roads—at least until newly-plowed soil had been exposed to the wind.

The dry wind rekindled old fears. I felt sure the point of no return had passed—the time when replanting would be pointless. I'd heard of late June cotton making a crop, assuming a delayed frost, but it was a gambler's crop. If the need arose, Zack would have the expensive alternative of irrigating an extra time, a luxury Daddy hadn't had, and then he would turn his prayers toward dry weather.

It occurred to me that the gritty feel of sand on my skin was not unlike that of salt. At sea, I'd often stood on the gun tubs extending out over the water. Each time the bow would slice into a moderately high wave, a mist would reach hangar deck level where the larger guns were mounted. But, whereas, the salt had been cool, this sand was hot and uncomfortable on my burning skin.

The only carelessweeds and blueweeds that remained were those that grew close to cotton stalks. The rest had been turned under by Zack's cultivator. I accomplished the weeding at a slow walk, stopping only for young devil's claws or tumbleweeds or an occasional volunteer feed stalk from last year's crop. Years before, I'd hoed Daddy's fields, suppressing my anger at having to work while other kids played and looking forward to the time when I would be on my own and would leave this high land and its fickle promises far behind. And now, working in Zack's fields, when I should have been looking to the future, I could only pass the monotonous hours looking back on the intervening years.

I thought mostly of the people and the relationships I'd recently left behind. And if there were any measure of the changes I'd undergone, it was in the effect of those relationships on me. And the suddenness of being cut off from those intense sharings of self left me feeling disconnected and indescribably lonely. Not lonely for the lack of some *one* near but for the particular *type* of sharing. I'd been told that friendships among enlisted military personnel were of a strength that might not be equaled in later years. I hoped it wasn't so. But I understood why it had been said.

Robert Abbott from Shreveport. Called 'Rabbit'. He could play and sing every Jimmie Rodgers song ever recorded, with each guitar lick exactly like the original. Soft-spoken, without an enemy, he never had a dollar because he drank it all or loaned it all away. His daddy worked the barges on the Red River and ran trot lines with his five sons every night. Rabbit (I never called him anything but, and he never called me anything but 'Sodbuster') liked to say that when he left the Navy he would put an anchor on his back and carry it inland until someone asked, "What is that you have on your back?" And then he would put it down and settle there for life. He had a narrow face with a sharp nose and straight black hair, and he spoke with an unaffected drawl, his speech laced with mannerisms that marked him as a son of the under-educated South—until the surprised listener realized that Rabbit's grammar was impeccable and the scope of his knowledge remarkable for his years. Rabbit and I had met in electronics school after boot camp. Many nights

Rabbit and I had joined discussions that lasted into the early morning hours, and we corresponded for a year after being assigned to our respective ships. His last letter had begun: "Sodbuster. Why, you sly sack of sheep shit..."

Carl Dabkrowski from Milwaukee. 'Commie' to his close friends—'Ski' to everyone else. His father was a professor of political science at Marquette and his mother was a teacher of classical ballet. On a long holiday weekend, Carl and I had violated the Navy's five hundred mile limit for liberty passes and had flown from Boston to Milwaukee. It had proved to be one of the more memorable weekends of my life. Dr. Dabkrowski was a gourmet cook, and his wife, it turned out, had been born and reared in Clovis, New Mexico, just a few miles from the Texas state line—practically in my back yard. They were gracious hosts. Carl and I, both avid photographers, took advantage of the season and captured the late fall colors in a day-long trip that took us nearly into Canada. It was he who introduced me to the more recent novelists, to impressionist paintings, and oddly enough, to bluegrass music.

Bill McClaren from Milford, New York. No nickname. Just 'Bill.' My closest friend for the last two years aboard ship, he had grown up on the dairy farm his two older brothers and his widowed mother still operated. When his own father died, Bill had been very young—but old enough that he understood my loss and, more than anyone else, had helped me through it. He had known nothing but the discipline of dairy farming all his life and had joined the Navy from a need to divorce himself from that atmosphere long enough to discover what else was in the world. But he couldn't stay away. When we were in port, he went home at least once if possible, and I often went with him. One summer I nearly fell in love with his sister, who was home between college terms. Her name was Julie, and after that summer I teasingly named her 'Julie Independent'. She craved the city—for theater, art, and music—and for freedom and variety. For over a year she had come to Boston every time the ship returned to port, even if it meant skipping classes. When I asked if she had any qualms about such visits and our occasional weekend trips, her brother being my shipmate and friend, Julie was offended, and I regretted having asked. The breaking up was gradual and painful and entirely my doing. The most difficult part was in admitting that I was not in love with her——that I merely wanted to possess that something in her spirit that was pure and rare. If the parting had been as painful to her, she hadn't let me see it. And when the final separation came, I had the uncomfortable feeling that I was returning to freedom the spirit I had tried to enslave.

But my friendship with Bill was unaffected by my relationship with Julie. Bill was my only close friend in the service who shared my affinity for the land. Our expressions of that mutual affinity took peculiar forms and were clear only in their lack of being direct. When I called Bill 'milkmaid,' he countered with 'field hand.' If Bill said that a man was a fool to try to make a living dairy farming, I said that he would be an imbecile to try it growing cotton. Aside from our rural backgrounds, we had nothing in common except friendship. We made discoveries together but, I was sure, experienced those discoveries as individuals. In San Juan, Bill had searched the city for an American hamburger. From the same menu, he had ordered his hamburger and I had ordered a Puerto Rican dish, and it turned out that his hamburger was more Puerto Rican than American, while my chicken was no different than that served in Boston.

I remembered others. Levi, whose every action confirmed all the Jewish stereotypes I'd ever heard. And Jody, who made me wonder how anyone could ever stereotype a Jew. Lieutenant Kerns, a lonely man, who came up through the ranks. A capable officer, he was passed over for promotion year after year until he was forced into retirement because he spent his spare hours fraternizing with the enlisted men and could never find his niche in commissioned officer society. Robert Gracey, son of a GE engineer and the best technician in the division, a reservist who had his own job with GE waiting for him. Robert grew up in the only black family in a white Syracuse neighborhood. When a job discrimination discussion arose, he grinned and said that he was "beside the point." Mark (the Kid) Kessler, from Cleveland, Ohio, whose humor was always wry and biting, who spoke with contempt of the Navy, of women, of Southerners and Westerners, of religion—who reenlisted. James Fowkes from Colorado, a student of the Bible, who never broke under the Kid's ridicule, who utilized the Socratic method in his ministry. One of my close friends, he spent hours with me, trying to tie my questions to spiritual needs. Anthony Hahn, Boatswains Mate 2nd Class, whom I never met, father of three girls, the oldest five, from Newark, who was swept overboard while fighting an electrical fire during a storm and was lost at sea.

And now I was two thousand miles away, chopping cotton. Unless by chance, I would probably never again see any of those people who for four years had held such control over my moods. The shock of being suddenly cut off from that intense environment had not yet faded. I was sure that David, in a combat situation, had known even more intense relationships. Once more, the longing to share those relationships with him returned.

During the last year, I had noticed an increasing tendency to become emotional at odd moments. Standing alone now in Zack's cotton field, the warm, dry wind brushing my back, the earth's heat burning through my shoes, I gazed over the rows of dark green plants bending to the breeze, the farm houses scattered in the distance, the unbroken horizon—and silently cried. I cried for all that I had lost. I cried for the very feel of the soil, for the nourishment it yielded to the crops and to the weeds and to my soul. I cried for Zack and his yearly cycle of faith and persistence. For Spider, dying and knowing it. I cried for my Mother, now alone, and for the knowledge that I could give her only myself but not *of* myself.

It had taken me until this moment to realize that it was not the lost opportunity to recount my experiences to Daddy and to David that stirred my emotions; it was the realization of *what* my experiences had been. I realized that, even if they were both alive, my newborn senses would be as acute.

Most painful now was the sense of *home*. What had once been my world had become detached, distant, and ever calling back. I could no longer look to my world for hope and direction. But here on the pale green underside of a blown cotton leaf, here in the thirsty wind, here under the high sun that laughed at dreams and gave the gift of life—here was my direction. Here in the place of my beginnings. And my hope was in the father-love that I had not lost, the mother-love I would not lose.

And here I stood in another man's field because I could not yet bear to feel beneath my feet the ground from which my soul had sprung. But as I began to walk again, to nourish this soil with my sweat, to turn the life of unwanted weeds back to its keeping, I knew that this, too, was home. And though I had no claim to its future, I possessed a profound link to its past and present.

SIXTEEN

WHEN I CALLED Melinda again, it had been over a week since our drive to Silver Falls. On a Saturday afternoon we made the twenty-mile trip into Lubbock for dinner and a movie. Melinda looked pretty in her white dress and shoes and it was nice having her beside me.

"Does it seem like old times?" she asked as we approached the outskirts of the city.

"Like old times but different," I answered.

"In what way?"

"Well, for one thing, you're prettier."

She smiled. "And you're not as shy as you used to be."

"Was I that obvious then?" I asked, laughing.

"All the boys were. Well, the few who asked *me* for dates were."

"I know there were more than a few who wanted to ask you."

"Now you're just being nice. But you know something?"

"What?"

"I sure was glad when *you* asked me."

"Me? Why, I was only a baseball player. I didn't even go *out* for football."

"Oh, silly!" She slapped me playfully. "We weren't as crazy as all that."

We drove into the city from the west side, and I was immediately struck by the rapid decay in that section. The drive-in movie lot was overgrown with grass and weeds, and the dairyettes and freeze queens where the kids had always stopped with their dates on the way back to Brodie were abandoned or were mere relics of the lively spots they'd been. Downtown, too, was less bright than I remembered, but its wide clean streets were a welcome sight compared to the Eastern cities I'd known. We traveled through downtown, and I was pleased to find the inner city still alive. The lack of easy-access freeways, I assumed, had preserved the peaceful dignity of the older residential areas.

At the old Preston Theater, munching popcorn and sipping Dr. Pepper, we shared Audrey Hepburn's terror in *Wait Until Dark*. When Alan Arkin lunged across the screen at her, we screamed together, and my protective hand deserted Melinda to face her stricken moment alone. Afterwards, we read the 'coming attractions' posters in the lobby and teased each other about our cowardice. It was very much like old times.

When we emerged from the theater, the day was still bright enough to burn our eyes. The air was clear and growing cool and smelled of the country rather than the city. I knew then that I loved this city, too, and Melinda, because they were good parts of my past. But whether I would cling to those parts of my past, I didn't know and wouldn't know for a time.

While light was yet in the sky, we drove to Mackenzie Park where the narrow canyon juts through the heart of the city. By the tiny lake's edge, beggar ducks squawked for food offerings from late strollers. A gathering of Mexican-Americans made joyful noise around an open grill and picnic tables across the water. Melinda and I, on the rock footbridge, took in the late reflections and the stillness of the coming night.

"I really didn't think you wanted to see me again," Melinda said.

"Why?"

"Well, you didn't exactly ring my phone off the wall after we went to Silver Falls."

"I guess I was pretty rude, wasn't I? I'm sorry."

"No. You weren't being rude. It's just that I naturally wondered how you felt." She took my hand and looked up at me.

"I felt afraid," I said.

"Of me?"

"No," I answered. "I guess *afraid* isn't the right word. I don't know what the right word is."

"There isn't one," Melinda said. "I've been looking for it ever since the divorce."

I shook my head slowly in amazement and held her close to me. "You're really something," I said.

She rested her head against my chest. The soft contour of her body and the light fragrance of her hair brought not reminders of the past but a special moment in the present. "I'm not a designing woman," she said. She leaned her head back to look into my eyes. "And in spite of the impression my mother tries to make, I'm not desperate for a husband."

"I didn't think you were," I answered truthfully. "And I'm not really on the lookout for a wife. It's just that—" Again the search for words. "It's just that it's—well, it's been a strange year and I've needed a little space."

"I know that," Melinda responded. "I'm not so wrapped up in my own life that I'm not aware of what's been going on in yours."

"Lately, though, I have felt that I've been too wrapped up in my own."

"You haven't been," Melinda said. "I know that you're concerned about me and my girls. And your mother. And your friend Zack."

"Yes," I admitted. "But still a little too much about myself."

"Well, let's not think about all that stuff now. Let's be selfish and enjoy ourselves."

"I'm a young old fool," I said. I kissed her on the forehead and then turned up her chin and kissed her on the mouth. "Do you think we're mature enough and emotionally stable enough to do all this mushy stuff and still keep our wits about us?"

"I think so," she said, "but do that again before you take me to dinner."

After I took Melinda home, I drove several blocks out of the way before taking myself home. I couldn't keep from smiling because Melinda's smile would not leave my mind. This relationship, this admiration was not something I had expected.

And that—admiration—I knew was what I found myself feeling now. Not that naive admiration people love to profess for victims overcoming their tragedies but admiration for the warm human being that Melinda had made of herself. She had overcome provinciality without leaving her home state. She had charm. I had never before thought of anyone I knew as having charm, but Melinda had charm. She had a way of touching my arm that had nothing to do with sex or even with romance; it was simply an expression of her warmth. She asked questions about me and my life that were not conversation fillers, that were not complimentary devices; her questions expressed her genuine interest in me as a friend.

The memory of Julie, the lingering doubts about letting go still remained as the hurdle that any new relationship must overcome. This night, during this side trip on my way home, I tried to remember Julie. I wanted to remind myself that I was not always in command of my emotions. Comparisons of the two were difficult, however. Melinda and Julie were two very different people. Julie had appeared at a time in my life when I was far from home and lonely, when we both shared and explored as adults for the first time. For a moment I recaptured an image of Julie—her athletic movement—her wild, long, sandy hair. I pictured her on the pier, trying to locate me among the hundreds of returning sailors lining the flight deck or waving from behind the catwalks. I saw her unmistakable little dance of recognition—and then the image was gone. I could not *use* Julie's memory, even in this way.

Melinda's appeal was something beyond my experience. She was feminine in a way that Julie might have thought artificial. But Melinda's femininity had nothing to do with old-fashioned servility. She would not allow herself to be dominated. But she would not withhold her feelings to protect her freedom.

Saying goodnight to Melinda at the door of the house where her parents and her children lay sleeping, the tiptoeing, whispering way we'd shared our cup of coffee in the kitchen, and our final silent embrace under the porch light, I had to admit, had been a little awkward. Perhaps it was best that way, I thought, because it certainly made it easier to keep the physical desires Melinda stirred in me under control. But leaving her this night even without sharing that kind of intimacy would have made the evening more complete had we been able to end it under less restraint.

But, when I finally arrived home and slipped into bed, I found myself thinking not of the departure but of the wonderful time we'd had in the hours before. I fell asleep easily and relived the moments all night long.

SEVENTEEN

A HUNDRED AND twenty miles away, Mother and I spent Sunday with Letha and Ozzie in the "stone house" in Seymour. Letha, five years Mother's senior, was her sister (Strange, I'd never been able to think of her as my aunt but always as Mother's sister). Ozzie Waldrip, her husband, had been forever a retired plumber and was forever in my mind a rocker and a tobacco spitter. The last time I'd seen them was at Daddy's funeral, and I remember Letha looking lost and Ozzie looking for a chew. I had never disliked them, but I had never really felt comfortable with them either, and I was now in their home for the same reason that Mother was: because they were "family."

Seymour was the hottest place in Texas. Everyone said so. Leastwise, they'd say, you *felt* the heat more. At any rate, Seymour held the record for the hottest day. When I was a kid, I loved trips to Seymour because there would usually be a reunion of sorts and all the first and second cousins would have the run of the place while the men sat on the porch or pitched horseshoes and the women, as the men would say, 'gossiped in the kitchen.' Thinking back on it now, I realized that the men had done as much gossiping as the women, but it wasn't labeled as such at the time.

Chuckie, Letha and Ozzie's son, was a high school dropout and a driver of dirt-track racing cars. Although he was old enough to sit with the men, he'd spend the little time he spared for family gatherings bragging to the kids about his racing feats or giving us illegal rides around the neighborhood in his latest unlicensed jalopy. We admired him for that and because he never wasted his time sitting with the grownups.

But Chuckie's twin sister Charlotte was a different matter. She divided her time between the women and the kids. But unlike her brother, *she* listened to *us*. She encouraged us to talk, and we were sure that she was excited about everything we had to say. When I was ten and Charlotte was eighteen, I liked to pretend that she was only adopted, so that I could one day marry her.

And now Chuckie was at the wheel of his diesel rig on some remote highway in the Northwest, while Charlotte spent a German evening with her Air Force husband and their three children. Letha, on the living room couch beside Mother, dully fanned herself with a Sunday supplement. Ozzie rocked and spat. Across the room, I listened to the clock and gazed from one lifeless family memento to another.

"Well, what are you plannin' to do with yourself now?" Letha asked.

After an awkward second, I realized that she'd been addressing me. "Get used to being a civilian," I answered, more dryly than I'd intended. Ozzie looked up from his tobacco juice can. Mother smiled as pleasantly as ever.

"I mean about college—or whatever." She spoke with a Louisiana drawl, although she'd never lived outside of Texas.

I squirmed. "I may go in the fall."

She persisted. "It's awful late not to've made up your mind, isn't it?"

Mother intervened for me, and I was grateful. "Now, Sister. There's plenty time. He can wait until registration day if he wants." That was true, if I attended a state-supported university, and I had already taken all the necessary steps to do just that.

Ozzie said, "Chuckie earned twenty thousand last year with that truck. Gettin' ready to buy a new one."

"Before we know it, that boy'll have his own trucking company," Letha added. "And Charlotte and Ted are comin' home in January. He's thinkin' 'bout gettin' out of the Air Corps and goin' to work for General Dynamics—in Fort Worth, didn't they say, Ozzie?"

"Well, that don't sound right. I think he said Dallas."

"No, it was Fort Worth. I'm pretty certain he said Fort Worth." She turned back to Mother and me. "Don't pay any attention to him. He never does get things right."

"Now, I know what he said. He said Dallas plain as day." Ozzie spat into his can and said to his chest. "I don't know why you wanta go ask me somethin' and then tell ever'body my answer don't mean nothin.'"

The conversation continued in the same vein. How Mother could have been a part of this family, I couldn't imagine. When I was still young enough to sit on Mother's lap, I loved to hear her stories about the family farms near Weatherford and Olney and Big Spring. And how her father had always gotten the yearning to move on just when things started looking up. And how they had warned her (ridiculed her, I'm sure) about the danger of going off to teachers' college and mixing with the wrong crowd instead of staying home and marrying Nathan Atwell. "They all thought I was crazy," she'd say, laughing. And one day she had said, "Nathan cried when I told him I wouldn't marry him." My little eyes went wide as hers grew distant. "We were only seventeen. I don't know what ever happened to him." I remembered that now. It was one of those handful of childhood memories that had always stood out in my mind.

And then a nearer memory came. The December evening after Daddy's funeral when the family had lingered until after nightfall. Mother and I in her bedroom with two of Daddy's cousins, until they saw that it was time to leave. Mother's family in the living room, talking in loud voices. Occasional bursts of laughter—until I, too, knew that it was time to leave the room. The heavy silence that fell in the living room as I passed through to the porch where Zack sat alone on the cold steps. Zack's drained face, his hand on my shoulder after I had persuaded him to go on home. The awful emptiness of the talk when I reentered the room. Talk not of the profound moment but of the past. The talk of men separated by the years, men with nothing left in common but worn remembrances. Talk that ended abruptly for silent intervals, punctuated by the clinking of dishes and splashing of kitchen water. And I remembered purposefully making them aware of my presence until they, one by one, gathered their wives from the kitchen and their children from the backyard and left me—as I desired to be—and Mother—as I knew she desired to be—alone.

Sitting here now in the front room of this stone house, I wanted aloneness. So powerful was my want that I chanced the offense I might cause and said, "If y'all don't mind, I think I'll take a drive around town. I want to see if it's changed any."

"Oh, don't mind us," Letha said quickly. "But you won't find much changed except for the big new houses out along the highway."

I excused myself and went outside, feeling much the same relief I'd felt that day at the Reverend Brandons'. But outside, as I walked toward my car, I heard the front screen door close behind me, and I turned to see Ozzie idly strolling in my direction.

"How're the crops comin' out your way?" he asked, clearing his throat for a spit.

"Pretty well. Do better if we get some rain."

"You daddy's place gonna make any cotton?"

"Might. Just depends on the weather."

He released his stream of tobacco juice and turned back to me, wiping his mouth with a handkerchief. He was a good man. For all the distance between us, I couldn't find fault with him. "Shoulda sold that place long ago," he said. "I advised him to many a time."

"There wasn't any place to go."

"No." He shuffled his weight and looked beyond me. "No, I don't reckon there was. Not if he wanted to go on farmin.' Land is hard to come by these days. You're daddy was a damn good carpenter, though—best I ever saw. He coulda made a pretty good livin' just doin' that." He waited for a reply, but I had none to give him. "Well, do you think you're gonna hold onto the farm now that your daddy's gone?"

"It's not my decision to make."

"That's true. That's true. But your mother, you know, she's lookin' for you to be a strength to her now. She's gonna need your help makin' decisions now and then."

"She's doing fine," I said. "I'll wait 'til she asks."

Ozzie nodded. "Just the same, she's got a burden now none of us know." He turned to go back inside. Ozzie's probing may have been awkward, but I knew that his interest was sincere. He and his family, as well as my parents and theirs, came from a people who did not divorce, who adopted the families of their spouses as their own, who looked out for each other. "Well, you have a good drive. Letha, she'll have supper waitin' for you."

"I will. And Ozzie—." He looked back. "Thank you for asking."

Ozzie smiled, or at least as much as I had ever seen him smile, and went on.

Except in very hot summers in the days before air conditioning, I had never really minded the trip to Seymour, in spite of how slow I knew the hours would drag when we arrived. The simple fact that the highway had curves and climbed up and down hills and canyons was a treat after two months of straight and level travel above the caprock. Towns were parched and far between, with long-deserted service stations and their canopied drives, too narrow for anything wider than a Model T. But the buzzards seemed more menacing, and I had always enjoyed that. And always I had been intrigued by the tiny houses, now roofless and windowless, along the highway—all stone, burned out or rotted-out, keeping their secrets. And by the abandoned highways that disappeared through the trees. Their foundations had proven too weak for modern loads, their course too winding. Yet, those I wanted to explore. Though they might lead nowhere or to somewhere people no longer wanted to go, they might also be parallel paths, with different, long-forgotten sights worth another look.

Seymour itself had an earthen look about it. Like Letha and Ozzie's house, many of the dwellings and business structures, built with the same native stone as those left idle along the highway, appeared to have risen from the ground. There was the old Rock Inn, midway rest stop for those on the way to the promised land of Dallas/Fort Worth. There I'd eaten my weight in chicken fried steaks.

Trees around town were bushy, their leaves dull-green but thick, hovering over dark patches of inviting shade. And any shade was inviting in the hundred-plus heat. But it was not a stuffy heat. The air smelled of wind blown through trees and over bright lawns. But today there was no wind.

I pulled my car into a Mobil gas station, tripping the bell four times in rapid succession. A teenaged attendant inside popped his head up at the alarm. He emerged through the door, wiping his hands and smiling like he'd just recognized an old friend. Over the door was a sign proclaiming this station as the cleanest in the state eleven years ago. I decided that it was still so.

He beamed. "What'll it be today, sir?"

"Fill it with regular, please."

Five seconds later the nozzle was in the filler tube and the pump was whirring out the numbers. I got out and went to the coke machine while the attendant attacked my windshield as though his life were at stake.

"Hot today, ain't it?" the kid asked. His number sixty-two football jersey fluttered loose and the shop rag in his back pocket bounced as he scrubbed at a bug spot. In my three years in Boston I'd never seen a station attendant wash a windshield.

"It's hotter than I like it," I answered.

"This is the hottest place in Texas."

"That's what I hear."

"You just passing through?"

"Visiting kinfolk here. I'm from Brodie."

"That's out close to Lubbock, ain't it? It's hot out there, too. But at least you got the wind to cool it down."

"That's what I hear."

I paid him and then swilled down my coke and left. I hoped that supper would be early. I wanted to go home. Ozzie's questions about the farm had been on my mind. Since that one visit before the rain, I'd only driven past it, noting its progress. Tomorrow I would go into the field and touch the soil again. I'd waited too long.

EIGHTEEN

"WHAT DO you have planned for today?" Mother asked as I dried the last breakfast dish and put it in the cabinet.

"I'm gonna help Leaman put up some rafters this morning. Then I might take a drive out to the farm." Working with Leaman Gossett was one of several jobs I performed on days I didn't go out to Zack's. The carpenter's helper pay was small, but it added up and would be a considerable help when the reality of fall came. Also, I hoped that it would make Zack feel less guilty about the time I spent working with him. With my savings and the G.I. Bill, I was sure that I would get by.

"Where is Leaman working? Out at Carl's?"

"Yeah. he's building a big tractor shed."

"My, that boy is sure going places. I remember when you two would fuss and scream at each other playing football in the front yard."

"I don't think Carl has much time for football anymore."

"I guess not. Have you seen him since you've been back?"

"No."

"Why not? He'd probably enjoy a visit. His wife is very nice. They sit by me at church sometimes."

"I don't know why I haven't been to see him." In my mind I was trying to reconcile the image of Carl in church, considering the Carl I'd known in high school days. "I guess I just don't know what we'd talk about."

"You do grow away from people, don't you."

"Yes, you do."

When I left the house I drove west, down the bad road

between the Mexican houses, going toward the flats. The stucco dwellings were yellow with the morning sun. A few copper-skinned children played in one yard. Across the street, a side door opened and a hard-faced woman threw out a pan of water. I would have been enraged to have been given her life.

Ahead of me, in the flats, the old two-story army-barracks schoolhouse stood as a vulgar monument to injustice. Discarded for six integrated years now, it still inspired me with the shame of my forefathers. In my first years in the Navy, when I was reading James Baldwin and listening to the speeches of Martin Luther King, Jr., this building had burned itself into my image of home until I wondered if I could ever feel a part of this town again, could ever look into the faces of its people without knowing a shared blame. I had never seen the blatant, open hostility here that was the popular portrayal of racism in the movies. I could honestly say that in all my years in this town I had never heard a grown black man referred to as "boy" or—except on rare occasions and usually then by brash adolescents—heard a black person called 'nigger' to his face. The subjugation I *had* witnessed as I grew up had been so complete that any more violent form would have been pointless. Here, where adults seldom ventured an urban profanity or shared a tainted joke in mixed company, white children were taught to be polite to their black neighbors so that they would not be reminded of the embarrassment of their color. Many times I had looked into the faces of the people of this isolated section of town and wondered if their secrets, as dark as their skin, would ever be revealed to me.

I turned at the street bordering the flats and crossed the railroad tracks and the main highway, driving several miles on the blacktop farm road going south from town. On each side of the road, the fields were rich with promise. I passed two low, rambling brick homes of the kind that belong to townspeople and gentleman farmers. One was new to me. Irrigation ditches were again being dug and filled with water. Rain was not in the forecast, and though rain was not yet a critical factor, some farmers were apparently not taking any chances. Zack, I knew, would wait.

Carl Bascom's farm was now bordering the blacktop to my right. Except for our preteen years, Carl and I had never been especially close. But I had always liked him. His father owned at least two sections of prime land that I knew of, and this half-section had been in Carl's name since he was born. Using his land as collateral, he had bought enough equipment that he now operated his own and several other farms. At the age of twenty-four, he was well on his way to becoming a 'big farmer', and while the old family farmers talked of his success with admiration, you could read in their eyes the threat they saw in his kind to their own existence.

Carl's house was a half mile off the blacktop on a county road improved, at his own expense, with caliche as far as his driveway. The wood-frame house was modern and attractive but not elaborate. I had helped Leaman in the building of it while I was on a thirty-day leave. Shrub cedars, already as tall as a man, lined the sides and back of the yard. In a few years, they would be a highly effective shelter against all but the south wind.

Leaman's station wagon was parked around back, Leaman sitting beside his thermos on the tailgate. Leaman ran a tight schedule year 'round. In the winter months he would sit on the tailgate until his watch said nine sharp, and then he would work non-stop until his one o'clock lunch break. His schedule never varied, except that during months like the present he was always an hour ahead of everyone else. Leaman had never accepted daylight saving time.

"Mornin'," he called as I walked toward him with my own thermos in hand. He said it more like 'mawrnin'." he had spent his early life in the piney woods of East Texas.

"Mornin.' Mind if I join you?"

"Shoot. Sit down a spell. You got time to have a cup."

"Looks like you have this job just about finished."

"There's a good mornin's work left. Tinnin' the top's about all we like." It was the first time I'd heard 'like' for 'lack' since

I'd been home. That was one of the reasons I enjoyed working with Leaman. "You and Carl are about the same age, aren't you."

"Same graduating class."

"Well, he kinda got the jump on you and a lot of other kids. Not that I blame him none, but I don't know how he managed to stay out of the service."

"He got married before they changed the draft law."

"Well," Leaman grinned, "maybe he wudn't as lucky as I been thinkin'."

"Depends on what you consider 'luck,' I guess."

Leaman put his thermos into the wagon, checked his watch, and turned to look over his shoulder at the unfinished roof. "Yeah, like you say, I guess it depends on what you consider 'luck.'" He turned back. "Well, you reckon it's about time we started drivin' some nails?"

I screwed the cap back onto my own thermos. "Don't reckon that tin'll stay down if we don't."

"Well, let's get to'er."

The hardest part was getting the sheets of tin up to the rafters. After that, it was a matter of trying to justify the difference in my helper's pay from Leaman's carpenter's pay. For Leaman, one whack set the nail and another drove it home. I averaged four to five strokes per nail the first hour, while he laid three sheets to my one. By mid morning, I was holding my own, and, except for the cleaning up, the job was done by actual twelve-thirty.

We had just put the last of Leaman's tools back into his toolbox and set it on the tailgate when a late-model Ford pickup drove up, stopping behind my old Chevy. When the dust settled, the door opened and Carl, taking off his western straw hat and wiping his brow, stepped out and came toward us. He was twenty pounds heavier than when I'd last seem him. If I hadn't known, I would have guessed him to be several years older than I. But his extra weight was firm, and his smooth, red face ruddy and weathered.

"Afternoon," he said, nodding, apparently not recognizing

me at first. "Well, hello there, Alan," he added, reaching out his hand. "Didn't know you were out here."

"Yep. I'm back in the working world. Looks like you've been doin' a little yourself this mornin'."

Carl took a long breath. "Yeah. Tryin' to get some wells started."

"You're not jumping the gun, are you?"

He paused to consider. I could see worry lines where his smile used to be. "May be," he said finally. "Just can't afford to chance it right now." He looked past Leaman and me to the tractor shed. "Don't tell me you're already finished?"

"Alls you gotta do now is spread a little caliche and drive them tractors under."

"Yeah." He walked underneath and examined the work. "This sure oughta do the job." He turned to Leaman. "You can tell Mr. Sims to just send me the bill and I'll bring in a check. Tell him it looks fine. Just fine."

Leaman laughed. "Well, now, I'm sure he'll send you a bill without me tellin' im. But I'll do'er just the same."

"You gonna be around town for awhile?" Carl asked me.

"Until fall. I'm thinking about going back to school."

"I saw you in town a couple of times, but I didn't get a chance to say hello. Been plannin' to come by and invite you out to meet the wife. She's gone visiting today."

"We'll have to make plans."

"Yeah. We'll do that."

"Actually, I've been pretty lazy about looking people up since I've been back." I felt strangely ill at ease talking with Carl. I could tell that David's name was on his mind and that he would not speak it.

"I hear you've been goin' out with Melinda again."

"Yeah, we've been out a couple of times."

"Well, maybe we can all get together some night."

"Sounds fine to me."

In the meantime, Leaman was closing up his tools in his station wagon and making ready to leave. "If you find anything you want done different on it," he said to Carl, "just give me or Mr. Sims a call."

"Yeah, thanks," Carl answered. "You can tell him we're still plannin' on that extra room as soon as the crops are in."

"I'll do that. We 'preciate your business." He looked back at me as he got into the car. "See you in town, Alan."

"See you later. And thanks for the job."

Leaman drove away, and Carl stood, shuffling his feet and looking after him. "Guess I better let you get back to work," I said. "Been nice seein' you again."

We shook hands.

Carl said, "Let's be sure and get together. And bring Melinda. Joyce will be glad to have you. We don't get out much this time of year, so anytime'll be all right."

"We'll make a point of it."

Carl walked away and got into his truck without looking back. I wondered if I should feel sad for him. But it had been an awkward meeting, and maybe I was making a premature judgment. I looked over at his flawless rows of cotton on the west side of the house and at the tall maize, already sporting uniform, juicy-green heads, and I imagined that all the fields he worked looked much the same. Maybe it was the pivotal point in the growing season that took the color from his eyes. Maybe success had come too early. Maybe I was all wrong.

──── NINETEEN ────

I WALKED FIRST to the lake. There were no terraces here. The lake was a constant, its face never changed except by the rain. And always the same change, always the same toads, the same buttercups and milk-colored butterflies, the same sweet smell, the same dog tracks through the same mud, the same still, brown water receding toward the low spot by the road. And always at the high edge, beyond the jigsaw-cracked dry mudcakes, the same clusters of lake grass with their swarms of gnats and mosquitoes. But the feeling was not the same. Not now.

This had been my wild sanctuary, my one untamed acre. Hidden in the tall grass, I could escape the carved and manicured horizon. Here I could rest my spirit with a corner of land no man could claim for his purpose. Here I could feed on the ghost of the Indian and the buffalo. Fanned by the eternal winds of nature, I could deny the shifting winds of change. But no longer. Not now.

Daddy had shared my secret. And David. Daddy had sat with me here on winter mornings, waiting for the sunrise and the blue-winged teal. Here in the extraordinary silence of the cold and black morning, I had felt his profound presence, his blood warm in my veins, his boyhood in me, my future in him. And only David had I ever allowed to share those moments. Only he had understood. Only he had run with me from the broken fields to the high grass—we, sweating together, laughing, listening. Only in him had I confided my pride in my fourth generation link to the Cherokee, my love for my father, my affinity for the land.

Now both were dead. Now I must park on another man's road, cross his terraces, chance his watchful eye to reach this sanctuary no longer mine. Its changeless face now smiled to me as to a stranger. I would not one day bring my son here on winter mornings, and he would not share this place with his friend. The world had been too much with me. And in this listless, unsettled period of my life, I could look to the past only to gain my strength, to find my direction, and to touch more keenly that which I had not yet lost.

Standing here now, feeling the dryness of the air, the stinging wetness of the still lake, I could only remember. The wild excitement I had once known I could now understand as the fantasies of youth. The pond was a lake only in memory. But the memories would always be alive.

Beyond the lake grass, I walked across terraces to the cattle run, up a narrow path along the west border that had once been fenced in to connect the barn to the pasture. Daddy's pasture had been only ten acres of the southwest corner. Never had he owned more than a dozen head of the mixed-breed cows he preferred, though in some years his small herd had provided the extra income that saw us through hard times. The short, rich grass here provided far more nutrition than that in ranch country, and with hay, cut maize stalks, and off-season rye, Daddy's cattle were well-fed. Daddy, I had always felt, should have been a rancher. He had a way with cattle. His succession of massive Hereford bulls were always gentle, and his cows bore fine calves. He knew when to buy and sell, and his cattle, always tending lean through the winter, were fat and healthy when they went to market. On several occasions, I had heard others offer him jobs overseeing their larger herds. But Daddy had never wanted anything more than to be a farmer on his own land.

The fence was gone, and B. D. Chester, who now operated the land, had plowed up the pasture and planted it in rye to be baled for his own cattle miles away. Compared to the cotton and maize on the hill, the rye flourished and B.D. would pay Mother a fair price for the hay baled on her land. But I missed the pasture grass.

I crossed the bar'ditch and walked up the dirt county road to the old house. The nearer I came, the more I was struck by its smallness, smaller than I had remembered. Except for the row of peach trees, some dead, the rest long past their fruitfulness, I realized that I had no names for the trees. Looking up at the branches, I saw that they had been pruned close to the main trunk, and I knew that the pruning must have been done in recent years. The house itself had turned almost completely the gray of weathered wood; only patches of cracked white paint remained. Years before, the woodshingle roof had been recovered in tin. Window and door frames had been removed and were stacked by the rear corner of the house, their glass long since shattered.

The front porch yielded to my weight like a boat in water. I could picture in a few years the porch roof giving way. Daddy had liked to sit out here after supper, smoking a cigarette and listening to the frogs in the lake. And Mother would sit here on lazy afternoons, reading until a car roared past, filling the air with dust and sending her into the house. Television having not yet come to the Plains, we would gather on the porch on quiet nights, listening to *My Little Margie* and *The Grand Ole Opry* from the radio inside.

I walked into the house, into the little room that had been my bedroom and the living room. It was hard to imagine that so much life had been crammed into so small a space. Now, only empty beer bottles and dog stink cluttered the room. The other bedroom was the same. There, the years without windows had taken their toll. Only scraps of faded wallpaper remained, paper I remembered helping Mother paste to the walls.

I didn't bother going into the kitchen.

Back outside, standing in a spot unprotected by the trees, I realized how hot the day had become. The heat was dry, and the sun struck my bare forehead like hot steel. Growing up I had always worn a hat or a cap. For a moment I could almost feel myself enduring a long inning in the outfield of a little league ballpark, praying for a final out and a cold drink of water. I remembered outsiders saying that West Texas heat wasn't so bad because it was dry heat.

I walked behind the house, into the back yard that wasn't a yard at all but a wide drive for cars, pickups, tractors, or anything else that could be driven or parked on a farm. The cement-hard ground was like pavement until it rained. Off to one side, under a shade tree, the old outhouse still stood and still stank. I remembered it as my family's shame and as the one reason, at the age of eight, I had been happy to move into town. And now it was the only thing that gave this corner of land the feeling of home—it was the only thing that hadn't changed.

I crossed over to the cow shed. B.D. had braced the old walls and was now using the shed to store hay. The cow lot, where as Wyatt Earp to David's Doc Holiday I'd refought the O.K. Corral shootout, no longer existed. On the other side of the barn, Daddy's workshop gathered age and lived out its uselessness. Beyond the workshop was the open field—the terraces.

I entered the dry cotton field and found that the terraces played little importance, as did the unfamiliar red Farmall tractor parked at the turn row. The wilting rows of thirsty cotton plants, the dirt, hot and powdery under my feet, the warm wind, the barrenness, the ungiven, unkept promise of it all welcomed me home. Here Daddy rested—not by a cold stone beneath a planted elm. And here was his tribute—not in the feeble words of a Baptist preacher. This land had battled him, scarred him, but had never defeated him. And finally it had called him home.

Standing now on this ground, I knew the ageless appeal of the land; I knew why men break the grassy soil and place their faith in a seed, a fertile bed, a chance rain, and their own physical strain. I knew my father's answer to the rancher's charge that farming was a defilement of the land. It was not we who drove away the buffalo and the antelope. Not we who placed our borders on more acres than could support our families. Not we who exploited the wealth of the land to build an empire. The Indians had been farmers but never cattlemen; they had killed the buffalo to provide their basic needs. I respected the rancher and his view. And I respected his claim to the expanses below the caprock, the rough country with its tall grass and meandering streams. But this fertile plain I claimed for the farmer. Few areas on earth were more adapted to farming and more productive. Grassland was plentiful on the earth, and ranching was not hampered by rugged terrain. Daddy, too, had used his land not suitable for the plow to graze his cattle. And it was not the fault of the soil that his crops had failed; it was good, firm earth, waiting to be conquered. Daddy had always been one hundred acres shy of success. One hundred more acres would have justified the drilling of a well; one hundred more acres would have kept his family on the farm.

I looked over the field and imagined again my dreams for this land. I pictured the patterns for irrigation ditches, the contours I would plow. Looking at B.D. Chester's terraces, I saw that they followed those same contours, and I hoped that he would win his gamble. I remembered Daddy's plans for sharing a neighbor's well and his disappointment when the neighbor's farm sold and the new owner, who rented out the land, would not listen to Daddy's offer. If only it had happened. If only it had happened. The land called to me now as it had called to him. The years of cursing these fields were all in the past. The endless weeds, the droughts, the heavy summer rains washing the topsoil down to the lake, the dusty wind, the lost summers—they were all in the past. What I had loved and hated, I now only loved. But I knew that mine would be a distant love; never could I put a plow to this soil that had brought my father so much pain. This land that would one day be mine called to me now; the brown earth, the distant dark cloud, the dream of what, with luck, could be called to me now. But I would not answer.

TWENTY

*Z*ACK WAS among the last of the farmers to give up waiting for rain and resign himself to another go at irrigating. It was the middle of July, and the cotton, now over a foot tall, stood uniform, full of small bolls but thirsty. I sat in Zack's kitchen rocking chair, an empty coke bottle in my hand and Spider, as usual, at my feet. Zack snored away in the bedroom. He'd been up most of the night, moving the irrigation tubes to the next succession of rows and resetting them when the time came. It was tiring work. At times it was necessary to aid the creeping flow of water along by spading small trenches from adjoining rows or by doubling the tubes where the progress was especially slow. Sometimes the water would break through the restraining dam at the far end, wasting hundreds of gallons of water and valuable butane, muddying up the turn rows and filling the bar'ditches. The awkward task of wading through the slush and picking up tubes to reset, between fifteen and twenty rainbow-shaped, slick, muddy metal objects to the armload, was the tiring part. Always, one or more tubes would want to stray in the cradle of your arm, twisting out of the pile, dragging across the wet rows while the thick mud tried and sometimes succeeded in sucking your rubber boots off your feet.

Zack snorted abruptly and the snoring ceased. On the floor, Spider raised his head and gazed toward the silence for a full minute. Then, stretching and yawning, he got to his feet. After a moment, he lay down again next to my chair, looking up at me, smiling open-mouthed.

"You in there?" Zack called.

"Yep," I answered. "'Bout ready for some breakfast?"

"I reckon. Soon's I get my eyes clear. What time is it?"

"Goin' on eleven. Almost dinnertime."

"Ain't dinnertime 'til you've been up awhile," Zack said as he appeared at the kitchen doorway. He was in his shorts and tee-shirt and had his khakis in his hand. His coarse hair was wet with sleep sweat, his eyes red. He went to the stove and turned the burner on under the coffee. "You check the water on your way in?"

"I just changed it. The last five tubes are in the maize now."

"That's good. Maize needs it bad. It's burnt like hell close to the ground. I thought I might get five—six thousand pounds off it a few weeks ago. Now I'll be lucky if I get two." He pulled on his clothes and sat beside me.

"I still think you might get five." Zack always underestimated how well his crops were faring. Five thousand pounds of maize—or 'milo'—per acre would be a good yield any year. Daddy had rarely gotten three and not often over two.

"Well, I don't know. If I'd watered a week sooner, it mighta just made." Zack's were not words of regret but a statement of the present situation as he saw it. Farmers learn early not to look back. If Zack had irrigated a week sooner, chances were just as good that the rains may have come and made his efforts futile, even counter-productive. And he knew it.

"Is there enough coffee in that pot for two?"

"Should be plenty," Zack answered. He got up and poured us each a cup. "Wanta go into town for some breakfast?"

"Might as well. I could stand a hamburger. I had breakfast before I came out."

"Well, as soon as I get some coffee in me and find my shoes, we'll go see what we can find."

We had Zack's breakfast and my lunch at Dottie's Cafe, across the street and down the block from the Lobo. It had been the original Lobo Cafe, but when the Lobo had moved to nicer quarters, Dottie Leonard's husband took a loan on his black-smith shop and set his wife up in business. Dottie had been widowed now ten years, and neither she nor her place of business had aged or improved their appearance in that time. The cafe offered the smell of good greasy food and good times. Dottie handled all the table waiting and money changing and her likewise widowed sister Emma did all the cooking. A yellowed sign on the back wall admonished, "No Tipping"—a warning that went totally ignored—and another declared, 'We Reserve the Right to Refuse Service to Anyone.' Though the lunch crowd was not large today, it represented just about every color, gender, and age in the county, but I certainly remembered when that last sign was not just a decoration.

"How's the cotton doin' on your mother's place?" Zack asked as he buttered his toast. He didn't look me in the eye for an answer. It was the first time he had referred to the land as 'your mother's place', and I was sure he had given it consideration first.

"It doesn't look so good, so far," I answered. "It hasn't grown a inch since the last rain gave out."

Zack nodded. "That's the way with dryland. Leastwise, the last thirty years it's been that way. When I first came to this country, most all the land was dryland. And the crops weren't so bad, as I remember."

"What happened?"

"Oh, I don't know. Some people say it's because we've done too much fertilizin'. Some others say it's because we didn't fertilize enough back then and didn't rotate the crops enough. I reckon the dryland's getting' drier, or just playin' out."

"What if we could get some water on it?"

"Irrigate?"

"Yeah. Daddy used to talk about sharing a well with somebody."

Zack took a sip from his coffee and looked past me before he spoke. "I remember," he said. "Would've been a good thing, too. 'Course it would've took some money. He'd have to've borrowed a ditchdigger and bought tubes. I don't know if his tractor would've pulled a ditchdigger."

"B.D.'s got it all terraced. What if he got somebody to go

along with him on a well?"

Zack looked at me and smiled. "Sounds like you've still got farmin' in your blood."

I laughed. "You may be right," I said. "These days it may not be a good condition to have."

"I guess not," Zack said, grinning. "For some of us it's about the only condition we got." He took another bite of eggs and bacon and chewed slowly. "It surprised me when B.D. put all that money on terraces. Course, he can afford to take a chance a little better than the rest of us. If he wanted to, he might try gettin' some water on it, but I don't look for it."

"Yeah," I sighed, "I guess that's what bothers me about it all. To somebody like B.D., a small place like that is just something to try and get what little extra income he can scrape out of it."

"Know what you mean," Zack said.

I looked around Dottie's Cafe. Her customers were the small farmers and the town clerks, the yard man from the lumber yard, the odd-jobbers, the tractor mechanics—division of class personified in the faces of men and women who struggled to make ends meet. True, the Lobo also had its share of hard-working customers, and Dottie's regulars sometimes crossed the street for coffee or a meal, but an element of the Lobo crowd never crossed over *here*. I liked B. D. Chester, but he belonged to that element. I was even glad that he'd rented the farm; perhaps he represented the only chance Mother had to realize any extra income from it. But for my sake, I would have felt better if its soil were turned under the plow of a man like Zachary Taylor Harmon.

TWENTY-ONE

A WEEK LATER, I sat cross-legged on the couch, filling out application forms and studying course descriptions in college catalogs. My decision about going to college, I still told myself, was not final, but I looked more and more toward it as an inevitability. My choices had been narrowed to Sam Houston State, Angelo State, and Stephen F. Austin. Mother had tried not to appear disappointed when I informed her that I would not be going to nearby Texas Tech, but I knew that she had wanted me to choose what I thought was best for me. My reasons were not clear even to myself, but I knew that when autumn arrived I would be moving on and that I would be continually moving on until I found the place where I should be. That any of my final considered choices would take me some distance from Melinda may have played a role more significant than even I realized. What I knew was that we both needed time *and* space—to resolve lingering personal issues still too near, to each discover our purpose in life, to get to know each other over time. Also I realized that my attraction to Melinda grew partly out of a selfish need to heal past wounds. And, without question, Melinda had, herself, been wounded far more deeply than I. I *knew* these things, but would I remember them when—or *if*—we were together again?

I heard Mother's footsteps coming from the kitchen.

"Well, I've got supper cleared away," she said. "Are you making any progress?" She came in and sat in her chair across from me.

"It depends on what you'd call progress. Right now, I'm just trying to get my mind into the college groove."

"It may not be easy after being away for awhile."

"To tell you the truth," I confided, "I'm a little worried about it. I haven't really hit the books for years."

"I don't think you should be worried," she said. "But I do suspect you'll have some adjusting to do."

"You know," I said, "what concerns me most is that here I am a month away from enrollment, and I haven't made up my mind what my major will be."

"I thought you were going to study engineering. I thought you were planning to continue in your electronics work."

I scratched my head. "Yeah, so did I. Don't change horses in the middle of the stream and all that. But when I look through the catalogs, I see lots of courses I want to take that don't interest me as a major, but I want to take'em anyway." I turned to a place I had marked in one of the catalogs. "Listen to this one. 'Anthropology 341, The Plains Indians: The Last One Hundred Years.' I'd love to take that. And philosophy. There were two guys aboard ship who were always arguing philosophy. One would say, 'Sartre says...', and then the other would say, 'Yes, but Descartes says...' And I don't know one from the other."

"You can't expect to acquire the knowledge of the world in four years of college."

"I know. But I'd like to do something really unusual—like going to college to get an education instead of just a high-class vocational certificate."

"Maybe you can do both."

"Yeah, maybe."

I excused myself and went into the kitchen to boil water for drip coffee. While it heated, I went into my bedroom for my guitar, then came back, made my coffee, and took it and the guitar to the back porch.

The sky was almost cloudless, much like that first day back home. What have I accomplished since then? I silently asked myself. All that time at sea I'd dreamed of being home—being free. I'd wanted to be close to Mother—for both our sakes. I'd wanted to find that David's memory was alive, that the town missed my father. Perhaps I'd wanted to find that it had missed me. At the city library, beside the plaques for Brodie's lost sons of the world wars and of Korea, I'd wanted to find a plaque for Vietnam with the one name—David Brandon. Someday, when the war was finally over, there would be a plaque if I had to put it there myself. Daddy would have understood. But his would have been a quiet understanding. Perhaps that was Brodie's way of understanding. Perhaps that was why I felt so lost.

At this time in my life, how could I concentrate my studies on electrical engineering? I'd been fascinated over the past four years by what I'd learned and by what technology could do, but my electronics studies had been devoid of human content. The complexities of invisible particles whose energy traveled near the speed of light according to inflexible laws seemed trivial compared to the complexities of contemporary American society and politics. I'd sat in technical classes, staring at symbols and formulas and schematic diagrams until my head swam. On the ship, I'd truly enjoyed working all night tracing down perplexing circuit problems and had felt tremendous satisfaction after repairs were made and the equipment was back on line. But now my world had more important problems to conquer. Over half a million American men and women remained in danger in Vietnam. The recent Republican National Convention that Mother and I had watched so intently, hardly speaking for fear of discovering new ways that we had moved apart, had weathered threats of violent social unrest outside. And, it seemed, every political movement in the country had already arrived in Chicago for the upcoming Democratic Convention.

My throat was warm from the coffee. In my hands, my guitar made melancholy sounds in minor chords. The sun shone omnipotent yellow through the trees. I'd given my summer drifting through odd jobs for meager pay and to an aging farmer whose destiny was to continue to live the only life he'd ever known. In my absence I'd grown apart from my mother's ways, from the ways of my town. I no longer felt one of my own people. I'd begun to wonder if I were still my father's son.

Abandoned Highway

For nearly three months I'd closed my eyes to my future, and now I knew that it would soon be thrust upon me. I had chosen to dwell on the 'what I am' and ignore the 'what I am to be.' But I had discovered that here in this bastion of innocence, this faraway simple land isolated from the burning cities, the anti-war rallies, the 'what I am' could not breathe, could not grow, could not be a part of the larger world. I knew that I must move on.

For all the resolve I tried to muster, I could not divorce my thoughts from the great questions of the day. The morality of the distant war, the mentality of those who pressed and of those who opposed it, the motives of the assassins, the anger and frustrations of the arsonists—all converged on my mind until I could not rest, could not be idle. I could not know that my conscience would not one day lead me into the ranks of the demonstrators, the drop-outs, the wanderers. I thought not, but I couldn't be sure. I had once wondered if I could without guilt return to live in this land that had attempted to teach me the sanctity of racial segregation. I had wondered if I could feel at ease with people whose perceptions I had come to question—and even oppose. I had wanted to find *change* at home, but the change I had discovered was mostly in myself. Perhaps some changes had occurred in community attitudes toward race, but I had long expected that when school and lunch counter segregation were discarded the white reaction would be unspoken relief rather than hostility. I heard the term 'nigger' less often now, but I still heard it. Zack used it occasionally, from force of habit, I supposed. But in other mouths the word remained the contemptible, derogatory slur that it had always been. The sad hope, I now feared, lay in the dying off of those who had grown old in the belief of racial superiority—the dying off of people whom I otherwise loved.

Before the specter of Vietnam, before I left college for the Navy, discussions among students had been exciting, even fun. Now I had no idea what that sort of interaction would do to me. Other veterans would be returning to school, some who could give me some insight into what David had faced. I would come in contact with protesters against U.S. involvement there. No doubt, there would be many vocal supporters of the war effort as well. Where would I fit in, and how much might I change? Could I let reason guide the change?

Aboard ship, discussions of Vietnam had been limited; discussions of civil rights had been long, sometimes heated. At least I had a stronger feel for my position on that subject—or, at any rate, for the direction I was heading. Old prejudices still lay hidden inside me and needed to be revealed so that I could explore them. Before, I'd met only a handful of black students in college. All that would be different this time.

More and more, however, I felt the restless longing for the sea. The sea was the master to change, not tillable like the human mind. If truth existed, it dwelt there in the deep. The sea would be an inviting master to serve, but to give myself to her service now would be to seek escape from the truths I most needed to discover.

TWENTY-TWO

IT WAS AFTER midnight when Melinda and I left the Carl Bascoms' house. What I had expected to be a dreary, obligatory occasion had turned out to be very enjoyable. Carl's wife was a small town girl from nearby Swafford (I discovered that I remembered her as the prettiest cheerleader for the Swafford Bobcats). Only a few silent moments had intervened between high school anecdotes, but the anecdotes sustained us through the evening, at times bringing us to the point of tears with laughter. But I knew that the anecdotes were all that we had between us, and I was relieved that the occasion was done.

"I'm glad we came," Melinda said as we drove away.

"Me, too."

Despite the hour, I wasn't at all tired. The night was clear, the moon almost full. Melinda lay back her head and hummed. We rolled down the windows when we got to the main road, and I eased my foot back off the accelerator.

"I'm not ready to go home," Melinda said.

"Would you like to just go for a drive?" I turned to her and smiled. "Or find a place to park?"

She smiled back. "Do you remember the place—"

"Of course I do. Some things you don't forget."

"Somebody may have beaten us to it."

"They'll be preoccupied."

"You *do* remember, don't you."

"Like I said—some things you don't forget."

Melinda moved closer to me. "I like being with you," she said.

"It's very nice being with *you*."

"You had a good time tonight, didn't you?"

"It was fun," I answered. "Most of the things we talked about I hadn't thought of in years."

"I wonder what you *have* thought about the last few years." She turned toward me. "You've changed a lot. When we knew each other in high school you were different from Carl and the others in some ways, but now you're not at all like him."

Melinda's serious tone took me by surprise. "People keep telling me that lately," I said.

"Tonight Carl started to tell a story about David Brandon, and I saw something in your eyes. I've wondered why you haven't talked to me about David. I didn't know him very well, but I know you were close."

"We were."

"I'm sorry," she said. "I'm really sorry."

Melinda's simple words struck thunder in my throat." Since I had been home, no one except Mother and Zack had said as much to me. I struggled to express my gratitude for her gift of kindness, but all I could say was, "Thank you."

The sudden rush of emotion faded as we drove along. I didn't know if David's death had further implications to Melinda than its effect on me, but I didn't require any more of her. If I could share a kindred soul with Melinda, I didn't know. I had grown not to expect that from anyone. Most of my life had been spent seeking a certain quality in others that would confirm my own feeling, not my opinions, not my interpretation of meaning, but my *feeling* —my feeling that human importance rested in the individual and his effect on others' lives and not in the collective attitudes or actions of groups. If a small town preacher's son had died in a foreign war, who could question why? and of what importance? But if David Brandon of Brodie, Texas—my friend, who had walked and joked and talked and shared my youth with me—died in Vietnam, the questions must be asked, and somehow answers must be found.

"Yes, I enjoyed myself tonight," I repeated. "Funny

thing is, I didn't expect to at all."

Melinda stifled a laugh. "I keep thinking of things that happened in those years that I wish I'd brought up tonight."

"What were you thinking about just now?"

"Oh, nothing really very funny. Besides, I'd rather relax and enjoy the drive."

"Melinda?"

"Yes?" She turned to me.

"What kinds of plans have you made? I mean, how do you plan to live your life now that you're—"

"Divorced?" I nodded. "Well, I only plan to do the best I can for my girls and myself."

"Will you be staying in Brodie?"

"Probably not," she answered. "I can't stay with my parents for long. I wouldn't feel right about that." She paused, and when I looked over, she was smiling. "Of course, they love being grandparents," she said, "but it's really too much for them and it gets a little crowded. I want to make a home for my children, and I'm not sure I can do that here."

"You know, you've changed a lot, too," I said.

"Oh? In what way."

"Well, you don't giggle any more?"

"Was I a giggler?"

"One of the best."

"Come to think of it, I guess I was. And what else."

"You've matured. And not just physically—though, I must say that I really do like the way you've matured physically—but everything about you—the way you dress, the way you speak, the things that are important to you. And what I've noticed most is that you have no selfishness about you."

"Don't be too sure about that. Sometimes when I think about some of the things that have happened to me the last couple of years, I just want to get on a big boat and sail away to some deserted island where I can try to be happy."

"I hope you know—," I started. Inside my mind I searched for words. "I hope you know that I consider you a very special person, and I want you always to be happy."

She leaned to me and kissed me on the cheek. "Thank you," she said.

Suddenly, I felt awkward, embarrassed. "My goodness," I stammered, "we're sure thankful tonight, aren't we?"

"I am," she said. "And how about you? Have you made that decision about what you're going to do now?"

I shrugged. "Well, I *will* be going to college. That's about as far as I've decided. After that, who knows?"

"You've still got a lot of things on your mind to be settled, don't you?" I didn't answer. "Alan," she added, "you're always going to have an unsettled mind. That's your nature. That's one reason I have so much respect for you."

Not turning to meet her eyes, I smiled an uncomfortable smile and drove on.

No one was parked at the 'old spot,' as we had always called it. On weekend nights during school months or after a ball game, twenty or more cars might be lined up along the dirt road a mile from town. Tonight, it was just another dirt country road.

I pulled the car to the side of the road and turned off the ignition and the lights. For awhile, we sat in silence, and then, gently, I pulled Melinda to me and kissed her. For a long moment, we held close to each other, touching, kissing, feeling lost in time. Finally, she lay her head on my shoulder, while I cradled her in my arms.

She sighed. "I feel like a high school girl."

I grinned. "You feel like a full-grown woman to me."

"Oh, you," she said, smothering her laughter into my shoulder. "You're right. I feel like a full-grown woman."

"A mighty pretty one—a soft one."

She looked up to me. "You're not trying flattery, are you?"

I brushed her hair from her eyes. "What kind of guy do you think I am?"

She closed her eyes and pressed her head against me. "A nice guy," she said, "a very nice guy." I felt her hand tremble in mine. My mind raced with broken thoughts. At this moment I knew that we were more at one than we'd ever been. Not since the good days with Julie, more than a thousand miles away and nearly a year back in time, had I been able to feel that with a woman. I clasped Melinda's hand so tightly that I was afraid I might hurt her. I felt her shoulder moving against my chest. "Hold me," she whispered. Don't let me feel lonely tonight. I don't want to make love, but just hold me, please."

"Yes," I answered. "I will." I pulled her closer and we kissed again, touching more intimately than we'd touched before. I lost track of time. Through the window, I gazed out at the stars. Wisps of hair strayed over my arms. Night air pleasantly chilled my skin.

"I wish life was always like this," Melinda said.

"I do, too."

"I wish it could all be holding and caring and not being hurt. And trusting."

"We can have moments."

"But moments always end."

"Yes, but we can have moments worth remembering. I care for you. And I trust you."

"I trust you, too," she said. "That's why I want this moment to last. I don't want to go back to being lonely, and I know I will when you go away."

"Why is everybody so convinced that I'm going away?"

"Aren't you?"

"Yes," I answered, "I suppose I am. But you happen to be with a very confused individual right now." I put my hand on her cheek. "Maybe I'll find something here that will make me want to stay."

Suddenly, she pulled my hand away. "Don't say that," she whispered.

"Why not?

"Because I won't let myself stop you from doing what you have to do. Because you're not ready to fall in love any more than I am." She released herself from my arm and moved away.

"I don't understand."

She looked imploringly into my eyes. "What you don't understand is that I'm a woman with two little girls that I care for very much. And right now those little girls are the most important thing in my life. Until I can make a home for them, I won't allow myself to fall in love."

I took a deep breath and slowly exhaled. I laughed. "Not even with a great guy like me?"

"Not even with a great guy like you, because I know that you have important things to settle in your life, too."

"Yes," I reluctantly agreed. "I guess I do."

We were both silent for a moment. I turned to look out into the darkness. Before this night I'd only wondered at the possibility of falling in love with Melinda. Now I knew how easy it would be—and how difficult for me. When I turned back to her, I realized that she had been watching me.

"What were you thinking?" she asked.

"Selfish thoughts," I answered, looking away again.

"We have to be selfish sometimes."

"I suppose."

"You know what I'm saying is true. You know you're not ready to fall for someone like me."

Taking her hand, I looked into her eyes. "I could really care for someone like you. I *do* care for you."

She moved closer to me again, and once more we held to each other. Up the road, I saw car lights headed our way and mentally prepared for the old response of turning on the headlights when the car came nearer. But the car turned onto the paved road to Brodie, and I surrendered my thoughts again to Melinda.

Ever so slightly, I felt Melinda move in my arms. She fingered a button on my shirt for a minute and then caressed my arm before resting still again. "I want you to know," she whispered, "that I really wish we could go somewhere and make love right now."

"I do, too."

"But we can't. I can't carry that, knowing that you must go

away." She looked deeply into my eyes. "I hope you're not angry with me for saying it. But I had to let you know."

"I'm not angry," I said. "And I understand." I kissed her hand and held her to me. As much as I wanted her, as much alive and free as I felt with her, I knew that she was right. Someday things might be different, but now was not the time. Someday we might grow apart and this would be just a beautiful memory.

TWENTY-THREE

WRANGLING A LEAVE on short notice had required some negotiation and trading with a couple of shipmates, but getting two weeks when David would be home had been important to me. He'd just received his orders to 'Nam and had urged me to pull strings to be there.

I arrived first and, at their invitation, rode to the airport with the Brandons. I insisted on waiting in the car outside the terminal so that they could have some time alone. When David appeared in the rearview mirror, I was almost stunned. I turned and there was David, in full uniform, carrying himself with impressive military bearing. I, too, had done my travels in uniform in order to qualify for standby fare, but my uniform was the bellbottom and slipover thing with the crumpled white hat. David's appearance was striking, with creased pants, jacket, tie, and a real military hat. David had always been a little sloppy and a little stoop-shouldered. This was a made-over David. The army had beefed him up a bit and put a little pride in his step. I didn't yet know how I was going to take it, but the change seemed to suit him well.

"Boy, it's great to see you!" he said as I emerged from the car. He put down his duffel bag and we embraced.

I stepped back, pretending, without much effort, to be impressed. "Man, let me get a look at this soldier! Would you look at those creases!" Brother and Mrs. Brandon beamed.

"It's all for show," David said. "Just get me home and let me dig out some jeans."

"That's the David I know!" I said.

When we returned to Brodie, David's sister and her family were waiting. I excused myself quickly.

David stayed outside with me a moment on the front porch while the others went inside. "Don't go to bed early," he said.

"I'll be waiting."

I turned away, walking out to the street. When I turned back, David was still there, watching me, grinning ear to ear. His uniform was still perfect—but he was beginning to slouch.

Daddy was in bed by eleven. Mother was asleep on the couch after failing to last through the late show. I gently woke her up.

"The movie's over, Mother."

Slowly, she awoke. "Did you see the ending?"

"I was reading. David's coming over in a little while."

"Well, you two just stay up and talk as long as you like. It won't bother us."

"Good night, Mother."

"Good night." I could hear Daddy's soft snore when the bedroom door opened. The door closed and the house was still.

About twenty minutes later, I heard David's footsteps on the walk. As quietly as I could, I hurried to the front door and stepped outside.

"How about a drive?"

"Sure."

We piled into my car. The starter sound tore into the night, but only for a second. I shifted into first and, at very low revs, eased out to the street.

"Where would you like to go?" I asked.

"Mexico."

I laughed. "Mexico! Are you serious."

"Very serious."

"What about your folks?"

"I already told them I was spending the day with you tomorrow." He turned to me. "What about yours?"

"I'll call them in the morning."

"I got a wad of pay. You doing okay?"

"Unless we break down."

"Let's go."

We had breakfast in Ciudad Acuña—huevos rancheros and a view of the Rio Grande. It was a first for both of us.

Before crossing over, we'd stopped at a pay phone. I was glad that Daddy answered my call. He was surprised but not displeased. David tried to hide his nervousness when he took the phone. I returned to the car.

David huddled over the phone, keeping his back to me. After a few frustration gestures, he nodded into the phone and hung up. He was shaking his head as he approached the car and broke into a grin when he retook his seat.

"Well, I just can't make the break," he said. "I told'em we were in Austin."

"Why Austin?"

David stared ahead, the grin still fixed. "One of Daddy's favorite sermons is about the sinners who go down to Mexico."

After breakfast, we spent the morning strolling the streets and gazing into the tourist stores. The night drive had passed largely without conversation as we took turns sleeping. During the morning our talk was mainly of what we were experiencing at the moment. I knew that David was holding back, but I was not going to push him.

We went back over the bridge into Del Rio for lunch and then found a motel and caught up on our sleep. I slept hard, dreaming of cheap leather billfolds and hot, wonderful salsa until I felt the bed shake and awoke to see David, sitting on his bed, pushing at mine with his sock feet.

"Whew!" I said. "We need to buy us a change of clothes."

"Let's do it quick," he said. "I'm thinking about enchiladas."

Showered and reclothed, we headed back across the river, this time, to avoid paying the policeman to look after my car, by taxi. We asked the driver where to go for the real stuff and he dropped us off at a cantina a few blocks past where we'd ventured earlier.

"Do you think this is safe?" David asked.

"Why? You didn't bring all your money with you, did you?"

"No. But I was wondering what the military would do if something happened to us here. I seem to remember something they said in boot camp about not leaving the country without permission."

"That sounds familiar." I never learned if it was true.

He leaned back his head and laughed the sort of laugh that we used to call a 'hoot.' "Here I am about to be flown into a country where somebody's gonna be behind every tree tryin' to blow my head off, and I'm afraid to go into a little cafe in Mexico?"

I tried to laugh with him, but I couldn't make it happen.

David made a fist and tapped me on the shoulder. "Well, how about it, Swabbie. You ready to tackle the hostile country of Mexico?"

"I'm ready to tackle some enchiladas and refritos."

"Then let's attack!"

The restaurant—or cantina—was actually quite clean and not at all threatening. Most of the customers were, in fact, Anglo—one hippieish young couple at a corner table and several clusters of young men we assumed to be stationed at the Air Force base in Del Rio. We ordered the first beers we'd ever had together and feasted on Mexican cooking until we couldn't force another bite.

The hours passed. At first, I sensed that David was a bit less used to the beer than I, but he managed to keep up. We finished our fourth, and David called for another round.

"Are you sure about that?" I asked.

"We're in Mexico," he said, as if that were reason enough.

"Yeah," I said. "I can't believe this. Your parents must wonder what's goin' on. I feel guilty."

"It wasn't you. It was all my doing. And don't worry about it. I'll take care of it when we get back." He closed his eyes and exhaled. "Man, I just had to get out of there. I couldn't breathe."

The bottles came and David held his up for a toast. I clinked mine against his. "To friendship," he said. And then he put his bottle down without taking a sip.

"To friendship," I answered.

"Alan?" For the first time I was aware of a slur in his speech. His eyes had a faraway look, facing me but seeing something else. "Alan, I'm scared to death."

"I know," I said. "God, I'm scared for you."

"Yeah." He picked up his beer and drank deeply.

"I wish—"

"Yeah," he said. "Me, too." He looked at me, grinning, shaking his head. "How come you and me never played football."

"We did—junior high."

"Yeah, but not in high school. And we were about the only two who never went steady with anybody."

"All the really hot ones were taken before we ever got our courage up."

David shook his head. "No, it wasn't that. We just didn't want to get into any ruts. Football was an A-one rut. Once you got into that, you couldn't even think for yourself. And girls?" He smiled. "Well, I'll have to admit, I did ask Janet Tyler to go steady once. Did I ever tell you that?"

"No, but she did."

"Oh, yeah? When?"

"When I asked her the same thing."

David, in the midst of taking a swallow, sprayed half of it across the table. We were both lying about Janet Tyler, and we both knew it. No way would we have asked that of the head cheerleader.

"You know," he said, suddenly serious, "this 'Nam thing is a rut."

"Why did you do it? I mean—" I shrugged. "I know I shouldn't even ask, but why did you do it? With your degree you coulda gone to OCS. You coulda—"

David held up his hand and waved me to a halt. "There's something you don't understand. There's something for real that I never told you." He stopped and was quiet for a moment. I waited. "You see, when I get back—when I get out of the Army—"

He paused again and I could see that he was uncertain about telling me. "—I'm gonna study for the ministry."

"You're gonna be a preacher?" I couldn't believe it.

"Maybe not a preacher—at least, not like my dad. I mean, I really love my dad, and I know he's doing what he believes is right. Maybe I'll study for the ministry and then go into some kind of social work." He looked me straight in the eyes. "The world is all fu—." He shook his head again to clear his mind and began again more slowly. "The world is messed up. A lot of people need help." He finished his beer and turned to call for more.

"You sure don't sound like a preacher," I said. "And if you could see yourself, you'd see you don't look like one, either right now."

"When you're around the barracks, you pick up a few words." He pointed at me. "Don't tell me your speech didn't pick up a little salt on some of those cruises you wrote about."

"Sometimes I disgust myself," I admitted. "But I left that in Boston."

Our fresh beers came, delivered by a very attractive, very young Mexican woman, dressed in a low-cut and short white evening dress. She set the beers down beside David's empty and my half-full bottle. And then she sat on David's lap.

"Whoa, now!" David said. "And what's your name?" The young woman put her arm around his shoulder and smiled back a broad smile. She apparently did not speak English. David eased her off his lap and pointed to me. "Sailor," he said. "Give you a good time."

I immediately put my hands up. "No money," I said. "No *dinero*."

"No *dinero* for me?"

I shrugged. She blew us both a kiss and went to another table.

When I looked back to David, he had drunk half the next bottle. "And, so, that's why," he said, as though there had been no interruption.

"That's why what?"

"That's why I didn't try to keep from getting orders to 'Nam."

"Because of that—that girl or my bad language or you becoming a preacher or what?"

"Because the world is in terrible shape. And I can't help anybody if I'm a hypocrite. And if I got out of going to 'Nam, some other poor sorry son of a bitch would have to go instead, and I'd be a hypocrite."

"But ever since this war escalated we've been gettin' new guys aboard who admit that they enlisted to avoid being drafted into the army. Nobody blames them."

"But you didn't."

"I might have. Who knows what I'da done if the war had been goin' on when I enlisted. Hell, I'm beginning to think those draft dodgers might be doin' the right thing."

"No, you don't."

"Well, I didn't until I found out you were being sent."

David finished his beer and started to call for another. I pushed my still-fresh one over to him. "Maybe you'd best slow down a little," I said.

"It's those draft dodgers that really bother me," David said. "They may be right about the war. Way too many people are being killed without ever knowing what they were fighting for, and what this country's paying for it just ain't worth it. But everybody who refuses to go causes somebody else to be sent, and some of them die."

"I think you're spending too much time thinking," I said.

"I've spent time doing a lot of things," he responded. "For one thing, I've sometimes assisted the chaplain. And a lot of the time the guys coming in are about to be sent to 'Nam." He paused and there was something in his face, for a moment completely sober, that I had never seen. "I've seen guys coming in who were just back from their tours." He looked me straight in the eyes. "It's not only that it's unfair that people are being sent over when they don't understand what's going on. It's unfair the way they're picked."

Abandoned Highway

Suddenly, I too, grew somber. "It's unfair that they picked you."

David looked away for a moment, and then he turned back to me. "They didn't exactly pick me, Alan."

'Stunned' was not the word. Stunned anger was what I felt—not toward David, though I wished as I had never wished for anything he had not volunteered. This, I knew, was what David had become, perhaps had always been in some ways, and I knew that he could not have done anything else.

I leaned back in my chair and looked around. No one was eating. Beer bottles and drink glasses cluttered every table. I became aware of mariachi music coming from a tape player on the bar. The white-gowned young lady was gone, but two other similarly attired women sat in two other laps. Smoke filled the room.

"In training," David said, staring into the bottle, "they kept sayin' 'if you do that in 'Nam you'll come home in a body bag.' Man, that sure built our confidence." When he looked up, his eyes were clear. "Do you think I'm crazy for wanting to do something to help people when this is all over?"

"No," I said. "I *would* be surprised if you became a Baptist preacher."

"I don't think I'll be a Baptist preacher," David responded. "At least not like any I've ever known." He held up his beer. "When I tell'em about sin, I'll know what I'm talkin' about."

We left after that and rode back to the bridge in the same taxi. Finding our motel took a little while. At noon the next day, we headed back to Brodie, talking incessantly of old times. David never mentioned Vietnam or the ministry.

This was not the first memory of David that I *wanted* to relive each time I was reminded of his death. But it was. The David Brandon who shared his junior high and high school years with me had been quiet but lively. His face had been the kind that smiled all over. And almost everything we'd done had been together. We'd played the same sports, especially baseball, hunted jackrabbits together, even double-dated. He'd confided in me his dislike for the restrictions his father had placed on his childhood. I'd had to go with other friends to movies and to swimming pools with 'mixed bathing' because David was not allowed to go. But when I had visited the Brandon's church, David had always been a dutiful son and church member, sometimes even volunteering to lead prayer.

When David died in Vietnam, he had just begun his second tour of duty.

TWENTY-FOUR

I AWOKE EARLY to the scattering of whispery raindrops on my windowpane. The curtain glowed intermittently to an electrical storm dancing across the night sky. If there had been thunder, I had slept through it. Drugged with sleep, heavy like stone, I wondered at the hour but couldn't find my watch, and the clock's unlit face was no help. "Rain," I told myself. "It's finally raining."

Seemingly minutes later, the alarm went off. This time I jerked awake. A ray of sunlight divided my bed. Outside, birds sang. I spat a curse for the dreams I'd had of rain. Burying my face back into my pillow, I groped to regain sleep and its pleasant illusion of the end of the long drought that had stretched now into the middle of August. But the more I groped, the more disgust filled my throat, and the more I knew that the hour of sleep had passed.

Mother's gentle knock sounded at the door. "Are you awake in there?"

"Afraid so," I answered without cheer.

"I'm ready to put breakfast on unless you want to sleep awhile longer."

Throwing back the covers, I swung my legs over the edge of the bed. "It's no use," I called. "The sunlight's already got me."

"The coffee is ready when you want it. I'm making biscuits and gravy." Behind the door, I heard her footsteps retreating down the hall and into the kitchen. Quickly, I dressed in yesterday's blue jeans and a clean knit shirt.

"You won't believe what I dreamed about," I said as I entered the kitchen. "I dreamed it actually rained last night."

"I don't doubt it," she answered, pouring my coffee. "It woke me up, too."

"What woke you up?"

"The thunder and all the lightning to the east. We did get a little shower."

"Well," I said, "I don't feel quite so bad now. Not that a shower will do much good. When that sun gets higher, it's gonna take what little moisture we got right up into the heavens."

Mother laughed. "My, but you're surely not the optimist this morning. Take a look outside. When the sun gets high, it will probably be behind clouds."

I jumped to my feet, going to the window. Off to the east, around the corner of the house, I could see a low opening in the clouds and the morning sun beaming through. Everywhere else, the sky was gray, not rainy, not especially promising—but overcast.

"I had the radio on earlier," Mother said. "The weatherman says there's a definite chance for showers later today."

"Somehow, 'definite chance' doesn't sound encouraging," I countered dryly.

"It has to rain sometime. From what I hear, most of the crops aren't doing too badly."

Mother was right again. Even Zack didn't seem as excited about the drought as I did. Still, I knew that the dry summer would cost the farmers and the town thousands in lost income and extra irrigation expenses; for some, it would be the last-chance season that failed, and after their disappointing crops had been harvested, they would put their farms up for sale or rent and call in the auctioneers. The hardy and the wealthy would survive.

I ate breakfast without my usual biscuit and gravy enthusiasm, totally dismissing the weatherman's feeble pre-diction. I had hoped to come home to witness the bumper crop I'd seen so often on the plains, selfishly desirous of buoying my own spirits but also wanting for Mother something more than a pittance of rent from her land—and for Zack and the others, something to give continued meaning to all the hours and the sweat and the tedium and the faith.

"I'm going to help Zack on his fences today," I told Mother over the last cup of coffee.

"You're not going to work with Leaman?" For the last three weeks I'd been helping Leaman Gossett build an addition onto the Methodist church building.

"No. We're all through except for some finish work. Leaman's a little particular about that."

"Maybe you ought to show him how you finished my kitchen cabinets. Maybe then he'd trust you."

I laughed for the first time that morning. "I really doubt that would do any good. Leaman just likes to put on the last touches himself so that he can go back years later and see what a fine job he did."

Mother laughed with me, but when the joke had run its course, her smile lingered in such a way that I knew something was on her mind. "Guess what I did yesterday while you were off working."

"I have no idea."

"Well," she began with uncharacteristic shyness, "I took a little drive into Lubbock and applied for admission at Tech."

"You did what!" I responded, almost choking on my coffee.

"Don't act so alarmed. I'm not too old to do a little learning. I think I'll enjoy being a schoolgirl again."

"No! It's not that. I think it's great! It just took me by surprise. Are you going to finish your masters?"

"Oh, no," she answered. "I don't think that would really mean much to me now. I'm just going to take a couple of under-graduate courses."

"That's great," I repeated. "What made you decide to do it?"

Her face glowed. "Do you remember when you were talking about all those courses you'd really like to take that had nothing to do with a degree?"

"Yes."

"Well, it set me to thinking that maybe I'd like to do that

myself, so I drove over to the campus library and looked over their catalog and—"

"And what did you decide on?"

"Well, I can't get away from literature, so I'm going to take one course on Byron, Shelley, and Keats, and then—. Are you ready for this one? I'm going to take an introductory class in astronomy."

"Great!" Somehow I was stuck on the word. "Why didn't you tell me last night?"

"Oh, I don't know. I hadn't really made up my mind what courses I would be taking, and I didn't know how to tell you your old mother was taking a step back."

"It's not a step back," I said insistently. "It's a step forward."

"I suppose. But, anyway, when I woke up to the rain, I got to thinking about it and couldn't make myself go back to sleep. So, I got up and started working around the kitchen and finally made my decision."

I sat, staring over the table at Mother, filled with admiration, feeling happier than at any moment since my return. "I guess the rain did some good after all, then."

"For me, it did."

"I'm glad."

"Wouldn't it have been something if we'd both been going to Tech at the same time?" She wasn't speaking with regret. I knew that.

"It would have been fun."

"Do you feel prepared for school?"

"I think so. With the money I've saved this summer and my G.I. Bill payments, I think I'll make it."

"That's not what I meant."

"I know." I had decided to enroll at Sam Houston State, five hundred miles away in the pine country of East Texas. I had decided to go undecided on a major, at least through the first semester.

"I think you've made the right choice," Mother said. "When you've given it some time in a learning environment, you'll be more prepared to decide what you want to do with your life."

"I hope so," I said. "I certainly hope so."

TWENTY-FIVE

D RIVING OUT to Zack's, I couldn't keep my eyes off the clouds. The absence of rain smell had me cursing, along with the undefined borders of individual formations affording no hint of cloud movement. Dulled by the absence of direct sunlight, the cotton leaves appeared darker and more full than they actually were. Purposely, I drove past B. D. Chester's crops, his own fields and those he rented from Mother, and was pleased to find that the cotton and maize on Mother's land compared favorably, considering its lack of irrigation. The cotton especially had held up well through the dry summer. On the yellowing maize stalks, small heads of clustered grain were barely visible above the long leaves. But the rows were uniform, with few gaps, and would probably pay B.D. for his time and effort. In the coming weeks, the combines would be brought in.

I would not see the harvest. I would be concentrating on my new environment, involving myself with new fields, nurturing new friendships as best I could, with recent memories. I would be lost in the pines, far removed from the blue horizons, lost in the process of learning, far away from the freedom of mind that I craved. I would not know whether that freedom lay ahead or behind.

Since I'd said goodnight to Melinda the night before, I had struggled with the question of what I had learned about myself. Perhaps time would tell. The miles soon to be between us would be a test of our new-found feelings, and the changes we would both undergo in the next year or two could unalterably bend us toward separate paths.

As I neared Zack's place, little whirlwinds began to appear

across the fields. Since early morning, the wind had been increasing, and now hot gusts broadsided my old Chevy, whistling at the windows and blowing dust onto the dashboard. Turning onto the turn row leading to the house, I maneuvered the car over the bumps and dried ruts, searching across the pasture to see if Zack had started on the fences. I sighted him up the fence line from the barn.

The day was one like those that had imparted to Zack's son immediate distaste for West Texas life—and like the days that had caused me, in my boyhood, to wonder if God had placed a curse on this particular section of his domain. As I walked from my parked car over to where Zack stood waiting, the wind whipped dust into my eyes no matter which direction I turned. Thinking that the cloudy skies would make a hat or cap unnecessary, I'd neglected to bring either, and now the gusts tossed my hair over my face and filled its roots with grit.

"Mornin'," Zack called.

"Mornin'." I strode on up to him and stopped, taking in the turbulence around us. "You should've told me the weather was gonna be like this."

"Somebody shoulda told me," Zack countered. "They say there might be rain in it later on."

"Doesn't look much like it."

"Well, you never can tell. This is the best cloud cover we've had in weeks. Then again," he said, grinning, " this is the only cloud cover we've had in weeks."

I laughed. "You're right about that."

Zack pulled off his cap and ran his thick fingers through his hair. "Hope we get rain out of this," he said toward the clouds. "If we don't get some pretty soon, it ain't gonna do much good when it *does* come." He put his cap back on and motioned toward the wire stretcher. "You remember how to use that thing?"

"I think I can manage. Let's see how much we can get done before the flood."

Zack's pasture consisted of only about twenty acres or so, but the fence was at least a mile around, jutting across his land to border the low, rainwater collecting areas and extending up to the highest point on the farm, where his irrigation ditches couldn't reach. Twice, rusty sections of barbed wire snapped when I tried to put one too many clicks onto the stretcher. Helplessly, I watched as the spiraling, contracting wire whirled back toward Zack, but each time it stopped well before he was in any danger. Zack would just look down at the lifeless wire sprawled over the ground, and then he would pick up the snapped end and bring it back to me to be spliced. Much of the wire should have been replaced. Zack was apparently 'making do' until the crops came in.

We worked through lunch time. At the time my stomach began to gnaw, we were at the farthest distance from the house. Zack seldom varied from his twelve-noon dinnertime, but I decided that today he was considering the possibility of rain more than he let on. The fence needed immediate repair—there was no denying that. The cows had already found several exits to the always greener grass outside. On more than one occasion, I had helped Zack drive and chase and cuss them back inside. Cows could be the orneriest, contrariest creatures on God's earth. We knew and they knew that they would eventually be driven back through the gate—but not until they'd had a chance to show us what they thought of the idea. I could only guess how much time Zack had wasted putting them up when I hadn't been there. One especially devious creature was a young bull Zack had bought to replace his old one. Many times when It would dart back into the field just as we had him up to the gate, Zack would yell after him, "I'll get your balls for that!" He swore that he would never buy another young one.

By the time we'd rounded the far corner and were halfway back toward the house, the insides of my stomach were raw. "It sure is gettin' hungry around here," I shouted back to Zack.

He drove another steeple into a fence post, looked up to the sky, and tucked his hammer into his belt. "Noticed that myself," he called back.

I laid the wire stretcher against a post and waited for Zack.

I was drained and hungry, dehydrated in the dry wind. Closing my eyes, I thought about the water spigot beside Zack's pressure pump. Zack came alongside me. "You must have had a big breakfast," I said.

"I did. Same as always." He motioned down to the wire stretcher. "Better bring that along."

"Still think it's gonna rain, huh?"

"Still think it might. Wind's dyin' some."

"Not enough."

We walked on up to the house, depositing the tools in the shed on the way. Spider's tail and eyes greeted us on the back porch. Wordlessly, Zack busied himself setting out cold roast beef and biscuits, warm cheese, and fresh-picked tomatoes, while I brewed a pitcher of iced tea. Silently, I gulped the meal down, not thinking much on anything but the food. Zack sat across the table as silent as I, and not until I was full did it occur to me that he had something else on his mind. "Think I'll turn on the radio," he said. "'Bout time for a weather report."

At the click of the dial, the last note of a singing commercial faded and the weather report was on. Scattered showers, it said, with all activity moving out of the area by nightfall. As soon as the report ended, Zack pulled a cigar from his shirt pocket and sat back down.

"They didn't say which way it was going," I said.

"It's comin' this way."

"We might get a little."

Zack spit a particle of tobacco into his empty plate. "We might get through with the fence before it gets here."

"I'm ready when you are," I lied. I could have taken a nap and slept for hours.

"We'd just as well get to it."

Deliberately, we carried the tools back to the point where we'd left off. The wind had calmed somewhat, and the few times I paused long enough to catch my breath I could tell that the gusts were less frequent and less violent. Cloud outlines now stood out against the sky, and, here and there, streams of light broke through, casting a glow over the fields. Zack hammered in the steeples almost at a walk, securing the barbed wire to the posts the instant I had it stretched tight enough.

Finally, we were at the cow shed, wrapping the ends of the four separate wires around the last post while the young bull's surly eyes followed our every movement. When we'd finished, Zack snatched up the tools and carried them into the tractor shed, then drove his tractor inside as far as it could go and covered the exhaust pipe with a tin can. I busied myself looking around for anything outside that might need to be carried in, still doubtful that enough rain would come to make all the effort meaningful.

"That oughta 'bout do it," Zack announced as I brought in the electric motor from his grinder.

"I'm still not convinced it's gonna rain," I said.

"We-ll," Zack drawled, "you never know this time of year. Sometimes it comes up all of a sudden."

"I know. I just don't see enough real honest to God rain clouds." Looking over the sky, I could see a lot of movement, but the clouds were hardly dark enough to contain the degree of moisture Zack seemed to be preparing for.

We walked out into the middle of the yard and stopped, scanning the horizons. I turned to Zack and saw that his eyes were fixed on something to the northwest. Momentarily, I was struck by his watchful expression, and I became aware of the absolute stillness, the slight chill in the air. I turned to see what had captured his attention. And then I knew.

"Hail," he said. "We might get some."

It was at least two miles away. Areas of red and green tinted the gray cloud. I wondered whose crops it pelted now. "Maybe it won't come this far," I suggested.

"Maybe not. Cloud's gettin' bigger, though"—which was Zack's way of saying that the hail was coming our way.

"Damn!" I said in a whisper.

Zack pulled his cigar out of his pocket and started chewing. "Want a coke?" he asked.

A coke! I thought. A hailstorm is coming his way and he asks me if I want a coke! "I guess so," I answered.

"Ain't gonna do any good watchin' it. If it's gonna come hail, it will."

When Zack turned toward the house, he didn't look back. But as I followed, I stole glances over my shoulder every few steps. Zack strode on up to the porch and opened the door for Spider. "Better git on in, old boy," he said. Spider dragged himself up and eased into the kitchen, setting himself down by the table. Zack retrieved two cokes from the refrigerator, opened them, and handed one to me.

"Were you expecting hail?" I asked after we'd sat down.

"No more'n usual. Ain't surprised, though, with them clouds reachin' up so high."

"Damn!" I said aloud.

"You might wanta be gettin' back home before it hits."

"Not until I see if it does come."

"Well, you're welcome to stay. I don't expect there'll be much rain in it, so you shouldn't have any trouble goin' home."

Zack got a store-bought apple pie from the refrigerator and put it in the oven to warm, while I made my first trip to the back porch to measure the progress of the hail. Once I thought it would pass to the east, but then a new line began to fall from an even nearer cloud. Back in the kitchen, I squatted on the floor, scratching Spider's appreciative head. Finally, I noticed a warm pie slice that Zack had placed on the table for me.

"Been to any ball games lately?" Zack asked out of the blue. He continued to amaze me.

"In Brodie, you mean?" Zack nodded. He was referring to the local summer baseball leagues. "I've been to a couple. We got our tails whipped both times."

"Yeah," Zack said with laughter in his eyes. "Reminds me of back when you were playin'."

"Aw, come on," I said in mock defense. "I remember a game or two we won pretty big. And don't forget we won district every year in high school until my senior year."

"Yeah. The year you became a starter."

"You're right about that," I conceded.

"Do you remember that game when you caught that fly ball runnin' back to the right field fence and the coach pulled you out of the game because you let a run score?"

"Boy, do I remember! But I didn't know anybody else did."

"I cussed that coach up one side and down the other after the game. You made the prettiest over the head catch I ever seen a Brodie player make, and that second baseman was supposed to signal you where to throw it." I could feel the fire in Zack's voice, and the old hurt I'd felt that day came back in a rush.

"I remember. I ran so far back I had no idea where the runners were, and when I came down with the ball, I didn't even realize for a few seconds it was in my glove. Randy Stilwater was on second, and he just stood there watching me. Coach Patterson had just taken over the team the week before and didn't know our system."

"Well, he should've," Zack responded. "That's the way Brodie's been playin' long as I can remember."

"I didn't even—" A sharp tap! sounded on the roof. I rushed to the back porch just as the hail hit. Millions of hailstones were already bouncing all over the yard and going rat-a-tat-tat on the roof. When I turned to look at Zack, he eased himself up from his chair. Spider was on all fours, twisting his head one way and then the other. While I'd been lost in a six-year-old memory of a baseball game, the storm had crept up on us. I felt vaguely guilty.

For over half an hour, we stood on the porch, helplessly watching the damage being done. At times, it completely let up for a minute or two, only to resume its destructive fury with seemingly greater force. I could almost see the cotton and maize stalks being ripped to shreds, the young green bolls scattering across the ground to die an icy death alongside melting white hailstones. Finally it stopped, and almost immediately, the sunlight returned.

"Do you wanna take a look at the damage?" Zack asked.

"I do."

"Let's go."

We zigzagged across each field and in less than two hours made a fairly complete survey of the loss. The northeast part of the cotton had taken the brunt of the storm—at least forty acres of Zack's best cotton wiped out. Another twenty acres had received degrees of damage, leaving about forty untouched. In all my years, I'd never seen anything more sickening than a cotton field destroyed by hail. In my lifetime, Daddy had lost two separate years' work to hail and had had his yield reduced on other occasions. Now, I looked over the lost rows I'd helped to plow, weed, and irrigate. Time, work, and money down the drain and no one to blame.

The maize had survived with little damage. I estimated that he would lose at least five hundred pounds per acre; Zack thought it might be less. If he got a good price, the maize might carry him through. If prices were down, he might go into the hole. I was sure he didn't have hail insurance. I didn't ask.

As we returned to the house, I couldn't help looking over the crops. Zack walked straight ahead. What was going through his mind I didn't know.

"I'm going to go look at Mother's place," I said as we neared the house.

"Figured you would. There's another hour of good daylight."

I went straight to my car, and Zack followed. I got inside and hit the starter. Zack leaned over the window. "It's a damned shame," I said. "I don't know what else to say."

Zack looked down for a moment. "Well, I'll tell you, Scooter"—a nickname from my early childhood that I hadn't heard in years—"I had an uncle once that was a professional poker player. He always told me that what you already put in the pot ain't yours anymore. You just play the hand and hope the other fellow don't have the better bluff or the better hand. The way I look at it, the other fellow's already tipped his hand this time, and I'm just gonna have to bluff him out."

I had never before known Zack to utter a philosophical thought. But it suited him well—or, at least, it expressed well the attitude that kept him going.

"Anyway," I said. "good luck."

I drove straight to Mother's place. The fields between Zack's and Mother's farms had been either badly hit or completely passed over, with hardly any pattern about the destruction. When I reached the farm, I was overjoyed. Not a leaf had been touched. Some water stood in the rows down near the lake. Farther up, only a thin crust gave evidence to any moisture. Twenty yards out into the next farm, cotton stalks were twisted and beaten. But B.D. Chester's crops had survived for Mother. Year after year, the same farmers seemed to survive while others suffered. B.D. Chester was a lucky farmer. That was the only way I could explain it.

TWENTY-SIX

O N SUNDAY, out of respect for my mother—and after learning that Brother Brandon would be visiting another church—I agreed to accompany her to morning services. Everyone was 'so pleased' to see me, as I knew they would be. The stereotypical portrayals of fundamental Christians were dead wrong in most respects. Though I might no longer share their unquestioning acceptance of 'literal truth,' I could defend them vigorously when they were ridiculed. My mother was one of them. My father had not really been, but he had faithfully supported my mother and had chosen not to question her beliefs.

After my visit with the Brandons, I knew that I would never listen again to the pastor's sermon unless it were at my mother's funeral. And if God were still listening to my prayers, that would come long after I had learned to accept that which remained too close at present. The Brandons had been at the First Baptist Church much longer than any previous pastor and wife, and, though I begged God's forgiveness for doing so, I hoped the time might be near when they would be moving on. I felt a closeness to them because they were David's parents, but I had always resented their interference in his life and in our opportunities to fully share our friendship. Surely they deserved credit for instilling many of the qualities that had made David the warm, caring person he had always been—perhaps even the qualities that had made me want him as a friend. But those qualities had been instilled early on. His parents could have—should have let him go after that.

The question that kept coming back to me always received

the same answer. Did I blame Brother and Mrs. Brandon for their son's death? No, I did not. But they had set him on the path that led to dying. They had made it impossible to question duty, whether it be duty to religious calling or duty to country — or simply duty to one's convictions. *Duty* had become a dirty word in recent times. Even Julie I'd heard, in the last months of our relationship, use it derisively, though I had argued with her that she, too, followed a kind of duty. David had never failed duty. He would find a coin and trace its owner. Once he had run over and killed a dog that rushed suddenly onto the highway. 'It's probably a stray,' I had said. 'Maybe, not,' he had answered. We never found an owner, but David had continued asking around for weeks. How much of that could be laid to his parent's influence and how much had been uniquely David I had no way of knowing. What I did know was that if such a devotion to duty could be labeled a 'flaw,' in David it had proved to be a fatal flaw.

"I wondered when we would be seeing you, Alan."

"Your mother has told us so much about where you've been in the Navy."

"God bless you. Your daddy would be so proud."

"Won't you and Mrs. Wilson come sit with us?"

Yes, they were sincere. Not a one of them did I suspect of hiding fifths of whisky in the back of the cabinet. Not a one was having an affair with his neighbor's spouse. Scandals, to be sure, had not been unknown. Scandal that I did not suspect might be occurring even now within this congregation. But scandals were rare, much more so than in the general community. If I'd been taught anything by Brother Brandon and his kind, it was that we were all sinners at heart. All men had lust in their hearts and many were under constant temptation from the devil alcohol and/or the devil nicotine. "Who among us has not...." No, we Baptists made no claims to purity. We sinned, but Christ intercepted our sins if we were truly repentant. And, yes, I was still a Baptist because I had 'come to Christ' and Christ never turned a penitent away and 'once saved, always saved.' By definition, whether or not I 'practiced' the faith, I could not become un-

Baptist any more than a mortal could become immortal.

But did I believe? Not actively. How could I accept this God who had all power and had allowed millions to die in two world wars and David to die in this 'limited' one? How could I love this God who demanded to be worshipped under threat of eternal hellfire while allowing famine and torture and David's death? Perhaps I could worship the God who had allowed my father to die because I could understand my father's death. But I felt smothered in the house of this God who had allowed David to die.

I sang the hymns, and they did comfort me. They saddened but they did comfort me. I walked through the garden alone. I held the hymnal and sang not loud but loud enough that my mother would know that I was singing. I sat and bowed my head—if not *in* prayer, at least in respect for those who were. I felt and cherished the community—if not the communion.

"God is speaking to our hearts," the visiting pastor said, and, yes, someone was speaking to mine. "Let us turn to...." And I turned to the page in my old Bible and read the words aloud with the congregation.

For an hour he spoke about the genesis. "How can these atheists—these so-called scientists...." That's where he lost me. For a time I tuned out. I searched around me for something to remember. I saw Daddy trying to adjust to his discomfort beside me. He stared straight ahead, but he was thinking about fishing. I saw myself in the baptistry and felt the cold water rush into my nostrils as Brother Brandon flung me down and backward before I was prepared. I saw Sarah Judson, blond and beautiful, sitting in the choir and drawing the attention of every school-aged male, and some beyond, away from the pastor. I saw the hypocrisy of pride in their fine clothes of men and women in this, God's house. But I saw the same hypocrites joyfully embrace and welcome the lesser dressed and call them brothers and sisters. And I saw David.

I forced myself to concentrate on the preacher's words. "When Cain slew his brother, he...." Not a good spot to reenter the sermon. The preacher spoke about guilt and innocence. Cain was guilty because he offered the fruit of his crops as a sacrifice to God rather than the sacrificial blood he required. He was guilty for drawing blood and, yet, he was guilty also for not drawing blood. If Cain were guilty of slaying his brother, how could that be different from the killing of anyone? If Cain had killed anyone, it would have been brother, sister, mother, or father. In the Baptist church, we called 'brother' and 'sister' all who accepted the faith as we accepted it. Our family was large and if we truly believed that no man had the right to end that which God hath created, how could we continue with wars such as this.

Good God, I wondered, am I becoming a pacifist? Or just a pacifist in relation to this war. I could not accept the idea that the murderous Hitler could have been ignored. When comparisons had been made between Vietnam and Korea, I had defended our intervention in the earlier war. We could not have stood by to let the communists politically enslave the rest of that country. Hadn't that other monster Stalin revealed to us the true nature of communism? Where would it end? But why was Vietnam different? Why, I countered, are not the Vietnamese as vigorous in their own defense as were the Koreans? And who are we to determine their choice? On other points I might have defended the hawks. On this point, I was angry. When David was still alive in Vietnam, I wanted everyone on his side to assure his survival. When he died, I had to wonder why our troops, risking their futures, could not count on all those they had crossed the ocean to defend—not that those who shared this country's goals did not fight bravely to the end. But obviously, to me at least, many locals called to fight for those goals were not committed to them.

I had sat in these pews before, waiting to hear words, explanations that never came. In those last years before college, when my eyes had begun to open to injustices that had always surrounded me, I waited for Brother Brandon to explain why we could not accept non-whites in our midst. Was it not that we felt, as some churches professed to feel, that *they* 'would be more comfortable with 'their own kind?' We had been taught that this was God's plan. After the tower of Babel, God had confused the tongues, divided the peoples and decreed that it should ever remain so. But who, I wanted to know, were the 'own kind' of the mulattos. And those of us, and we were many, in the church who had Indian blood—darker, Asian if we were to believe the scholars—what about us? How could we glorify Truth and still honor this lie of 'separate but equal?' We knew there was no equality in our schools, in our churches, in our opportunities. If there were sins of omission—and certainly not accepting the responsibility to right this wrong was an omission—why did we not face up to them, confess those sins and practice our conviction that all were precious in His sight?

As our spiritual leader today, guide us in understanding these important questions. Tell us not of why Cain slew Abel. Tell us why James Earl Ray slew Martin Luther King. Tell us why Sirhan Sirhan slew Robert Kennedy. Tell us why across this country affluent white kids are torching their draft cards and impoverished blacks are torching their hopes. Tell us why our loving, all-knowing, all-powerful God who created light out of darkness does not put a stop to this. I did not want to be an unbelieving outsider, but I needed answers I could accept as true—answers that would bring me hope and those who suffered so unnecessarily, peace.

Our guest pastor, of course, did not provide those answers. But as the sermon came to a close, he asked God to answer our questions and bring us closer to Him. I had asked too much. Neither Brother Brandon nor this man could give me hope and peace. I knew of no one who could.

We stood for the closing hymn. "Just as I am without one plea," I sang, though I had not one but many pleas. "I know there is someone out there to whom God is speaking, asking you to rededicate your life to his service," the pastor intoned. A face turned in my direction, in prayer I knew. Would Alan Wilson be coming back to Christ today? Had I ever left? The Christ I chose to accept years back was the Truth and the Light. If that was still Christ, I worshipped Christ. If God was still Love, I worshipped God. But if Christ and God were limited to those I had heard described today and all the days I had spent in this church, I would not be coming back to *those* immortal beings today.

Behind me, I heard the rustle of skirts, the shuffling of feet. While 'one last time' we repeated the final verse, a young boy, high school age, moved uncertainly down the aisle. The preacher met him and they bowed in prayer, while the congregation, without prompt, again sang the verse one last time. When it was all over, almost a hundred stood in line to offer this convert the right hand of Christian fellowship. Not to have joined Mother in line would have been too conspicuous. I did not consider myself a hypocrite because I was still a member here. I shook his hand and welcomed him into membership in my mother's church.

Outside, I spoke to many old members. A number of them I had seen in town since I'd been back. Of those I'd not seen, some spoke to me about David. Almost all spoke to me of my father. 'I've known your daddy since...." "Just the other day, I remembered when your daddy...." "It just doesn't seem right that your daddy didn't live to...." I thanked them all because they were all sincere. Their warmth comforted me. Perhaps that was why I had come.

"Before we go home," I said to Mother when I had a chance to speak privately with her, "I want to go to the cemetery." It would be the first time.

"Do you want to take me home first so that you can be alone? I can walk back."

"No," I said. "I want you to come."

"You'll want to spend some time alone at David's grave." She was being blunt, but she had to say it.

"No," I answered. "This time is for Daddy."

In all the time since my return, I'd been torn by the fact of Daddy's not physically *being* here. Yet Daddy *was* in my heart and in my memory. He was in my relationships with those who had shared his time on this earth. But I would not be near him until I stood over the stone that bore his name. I drove straight to the spot where the limousine had parked that horrible day. I held open the door of my old Chevy for Mother and together we walked among the graves. I truly felt Daddy's presence somewhere near, just out of sight, just out of reach, hoping that I had prepared myself for the letters and numbers carved on its face: 'husband and father, Roy Franklin Wilson, February 4, 1906 to December 17, 1967.' That part I was prepared for. But I had forgotten, if I had known, that this would be a double stone. To the right of those words, I read: 'wife and mother, Wilma Elizabeth Wilson, March 4, 1910 to.' Thoughts and emotions and memories stormed past my consciousness. Mother touched my shoulder and together we knelt before my father's name. I leaned over and rested my arms and my forehead on the smooth gray marble. The tears streamed down my face and dropped to the letters, collecting in their depths. Mother embraced me and then I heard her standing and the soft sound of her footsteps retreating on the dry grass. I renewed the pledges I had made over his coffin. I spoke aloud to him about things I did not remember later. And then I whispered, "I love you, Daddy" and stood to face my mother waiting by the car. I had not cried audibly. I had not lost control to the extent that I had thought I might. Out of that fear I had delayed my coming until now. But the summer had conditioned me for the moment.

When I approached the car, mother reached inside for the tissue box on the dash, then held it out to me. I took the box. After taking a tissue and wiping the moisture from my eyes I saw that Mother was not expecting me to open the door for her yet.

"Point out David's grave," I said.

"Over there," she said, pointing. "Against the fence. There's no stone yet, but you'll see the flag and the flowers. Mrs. Brandon comes almost every day." She embraced me again and then she turned. "I'll wait in the car," she said. "Take as long as you need."

I carried the box of tissues with me as I walked between the tall old stones on that side of the cemetery. David's small marker and its decorations came into view as I passed the large marker of Brodie's last surviving Civil War veteran, with its weathered message barely readable. I leaned against the Civil War stone and shook my head. "No," I cried. "No." I reached down and picked up a pebble. My first impulse was to throw it at David's marker—to make his death go away—to strike out even at David for putting himself in harm's way. It was Mrs. Brandon's flowers that stopped me. And the flag that David had died for, that I still believed in and would die for under different circumstances. I dropped the pebble at my feet, and then I turned and went back to the car.

I sat silently for several minutes after putting the key into the ignition. "Wait just a minute," I said to Mother. I got out and walked back to Daddy's grave. At the stone, I searched for something in my pocket to leave, something of me to stay with Daddy while I was gone. I found nothing personal but a cheap guitar pick. But I remembered that Daddy had bought me my first guitar when I had expressed an interest in music. I had wanted drums—I was nine or ten—but Daddy wanted something less noisy. He used to listen to me sometimes when I played. Sometimes I heard him humming when I chorded a familiar tune. I pushed the pick into the narrow space that separated stone from earth. When I looked up, I was gazing across to David's marker and I felt that bond that tied we three together. I saw in David's temporary marker and it's flag and flowers a transition between Daddy's time and my future. The world that Daddy knew would never return. The events that had taken David and thousands of others were not over and I could not know how long they would last. What I did know was that this was a pivotal time in my nation's history and in my own. I and millions of my generation and, perhaps, of generations to come, would never be able to trust with absolute confidence the institutions that my father's generation had relied upon. My faith in my country had been shaken but held firm; my religious faith could never be as it had been before, if it returned at all.

TWENTY-SEVEN

O F ALL MY memories of Julie, the most vivid has to be of the day we were scheduled to meet in New York City, a day that happened to coincide with the expected-to-be largest anti-Vietnam War demonstration in history. At three in the afternoon, we were to meet on Times Square at the point of that oddly shaped building made famous by the descending ball each New Year's Day. There could be no mistaking the meeting place, and if either of us were late, we agreed that it would be I, considering the fact that I was at the mercy of a 40,000 ton ship, which was at the mercy of unpredictable seas and the whims of the United States Navy.

The day before docking in New York Harbor, the crew were informed of the massive war demonstration planned for that day and of the rumor, spreading among the demonstrators that we were returning from Vietnam with several thousand soldiers. In fact, we had spent the last several weeks cruising the Caribbean and hitting ports like San Juan and St. Thomas—the best duty we'd had since I'd been aboard.

No liberties were to be canceled, much to my relief, but our orders were to duck out of sight and avoid confrontation whenever we observed protesters headed our way. It would be a game, it seemed, and one I looked forward to. It would certainly be something to share with Julie. I'd never seen a real protester in action, except on TV.

Bill would walk with me as far as Times Square, to say hello to his sister before heading to the USO to see what tickets might be available. Julie and I had no particular plans beyond meeting at three. We both preferred it that way. But having recently made

E-5, Electronics Technician Second Class (same level as a buck sergeant, as I always had to explain to the landlubbers back home), this would be my first overnight liberty away from home port. Julie had written back "Hmmmm," when I'd mailed her the news.

The ship sailed under the Verrazano Narrows bridge at ten in the morning and passed the Statue of Liberty about a half hour later. By noon, we were tied up and secure. To our surprise, the only colorfully clothed people awaiting our arrival were not tie-dyed protesters, but two young women who obviously sensed unlimited opportunity in the arrival of nearly three thousand sailors who had been two months away from home port.

The only excitement we experienced upon arrival was the presence of the Queen Mary docked alongside. Bill, always the frugal one, wanted to eat noon chow aboard and save a little expense, but I was anxious to be ashore. I insisted on treating him to the first hot pastrami sandwich we spied on the beach (off the ship) and, after making our two salutes—Officer of the Deck and flag—we were on pavement.

I'd been in this city on several recent occasions, but this was to be my first experience away from the bright lights and famous landmarks. All we knew was which direction to walk. This area might be scary at night, but in the bright light of day it should just be a dull stroll to somewhere more inviting. More inviting to Bill would be, I suspected, playing gin rummy with the nice USO girls or catching the latest John Wayne flick. Once he hit a USO, he was set for a few hours, so if Julie were so inclined, we might meet him there, pick up whatever tickets we could, and catch a real show, one on Broadway that we couldn't afford without a little help from our friends at the USO. I didn't mind sharing Julie with her brother for the first part of the evening. We would have another glorious eight hours together before I stood for the next morning's quarters.

We did manage to find a stand-while-you-eat place, something I'd never encountered back home, and gorged down a hot pastrami sandwich apiece. I never stopped missing Texas barbecue and Tex-Mex enchiladas, but the big Eastern cities included among their multitudes, as Julie put it, "purveyors of the delectable delights" of at least five—maybe six—continents. I never wanted for something tasty in Boston or New York.

Back on the street, with that greasy-warm satisfaction accented by periodic beer-belches, we continued on our mission. But a few blocks beyond the pastramis, we were somewhat jolted by the sudden appearance of what must have been about a thousand bearded, sandled, placard-waving peace lovers bearing straight toward us. They'd turned a corner at a fast march a half-block ahead. It was like seeing a crowd of movie extras costumed for a scene in an epic film. Only this, I knew, was the real thing.

We had just strolled under the awning of a greeting card and gift shop. Immediately, I tugged at Bill's dress blues and we were inside looking out, apparently before the marchers had a chance to spot us. We stayed away from the window, with nothing between us and the protesters but a broad expanse of glass. An especially bright sun in sharp contrast to the store's lighting, however, was to our advantage. Still the drama and the tension were real. I don't believe either of us were nervous. Although we weren't always gung ho about military attitudes, we did take our orders to avoid confrontations seriously. We had seen anti-war activists on the TV news: angry mothers and college students shouting at bayoneted, disciplined lines of scared young draftees, pacifists placing flowers in the barrels of pointed rifles. In confronting enlisted and drafted non-coms, the demonstrators, I knew, were addressing their anger to the wrong audience, and I was certainly the wrong audience this day.

As the marchers strode past, face after determined face came into focus. This was no college party—no neighborhood gang bent on destruction. These were not the cowardly, unpatriotic youth that the politicians and Legionnaires nightly railed against on the late news. These were the potential victims but also the parents, sisters, brothers, wives, lovers who clearly saw *this* war as a horrible, tragic mistake. The message of their countenance was not 'we defy the perpetrators of this great crime' but was instead 'come join us and help us put an end to this madness.'

I was not there in spirit. Not yet. Maybe I would never be completely there. The message, however, was not lost. But how could I completely share their sentiment? David was over there. He did not write to me with anger. He had earned my support and I was not inclined to betray him, regardless of how sincere these people before me might be.

Bill and I did not look at each other until the pageant was over. By then our eyes had become accustomed to the light. We were now sailors on liberty in a tourist shop in the big city. Here were hello-from-NYC cards for the folks back home, charm bracelets for the waiting girlfriend or the little sister. We looked toward the clerks and the few other customers—who did not look back at us. We offered our regrets to the merchandise and continued on our way.

Crossing an intersection a little later, we could see the same or another parade crossing a street many blocks away. But that was the last we saw of demonstrations. It was barely two when we arrived at Times Square, so, at Bill's urging, I accompanied him to the USO to make a quick check of the freebies. I had coffee with Bill and a couple of friends we ran into, but I could not get interested in combing through show lists and sightseeing schedules. It might be too early to meet Julie, but I couldn't wait around any longer. I told Bill not to expect us but that we might come by later to see if he were around.

Julie was still not there. Not at three. Not at three-thirty. I didn't worry. She might have been unavoidably delayed. This was, after all, New York, New York. And, knowing Julie, she might have dropped in at some art gallery or bookstore to pass a little time. *"Hope you don't mind. They had a wonderful collection of impressionists!"* No, I wouldn't mind. But I did begin to worry when four o'clock came and went.

Several times I saw shipmates strolling toward me. At first I waved or smiled. Some of them knew why I was there. After that I began turning my face away or ducking into the crowds. At four-thirty I started walking—never far—usually keeping the intersection in sight.

At five, I walked quickly back to the USO. Bill was not there. I went to the desk and asked if anyone had called with a message for someone from my ship. Yes, I was informed, and my heart thumped. I followed an eager young lady to another desk to look for the message. "Are you Gunner's Mate Bennie Brierson?"

My hopes dashed, I crammed a couple of finger sandwiches down my throat, swilled a glass of coke, made a head stop, and hurried back to Times Square. At six-thirty I left long enough to find a portable cup of coffee. At seven I bought a hot dog and another cup of coffee off a cart.

I did not think of leaving. She would arrive. At some hour, at some minute, she would simply appear. But I did let myself grow angry. She must know that I would be here until she arrived. She must know how long time dragged while one waited not knowing how long the wait would be. I reminded myself that I never had felt that I was really in love with her nor did I feel that she were in love with me. At least, I had never felt that I had any claim on her or that she desired a claim on me. Had I ever felt that Julie were seeking a life partner, maybe I would have allowed myself to be 'in love'. But I 'loved' her and I longed to be with her. Times with her were the most precious I had ever known. Being angry with Julie, I could see into the selfish side of her. Her search for life was more important than anyone's feelings. I *knew* but Julie *felt* that youth was a passing thing. To me, youth was only one of the stages one passes through on the way to some kind of fulfillment that comes after a lifetime of stages. But Julie was driven by the urgency of her youth. She sought change—not for the sake of change but because only through change could she grow.

Just before eight, I saw her. She was in jeans and a long-sleeved white cotton shirt—not the dressy kind but the soft, thick, off-white kind. She had a small button, red, white and blue. It said 'Peace'. Her hair seemed longer than when I'd last seen her. She carried no purse, but some kind of bag was attached to the belt at her waist. Approaching at a brisk walk, she slowed to careful, cautious steps, her hands locked behind her back, when she came near. She stopped three feet away.

"Hi," she said with one of those quick smiles that curl and then drop.

"Hi,' I responded with an involuntary shrug. The echo of my voice was not cold but not warm.

"I'm a little late."

I brought up my wrist and pretended to look at my watch. "Yes," I said. "a little bit."

"I'm sorry," she said. "You must be really tired from standing here."

"A little," I said. "I walked around some."

"I was here just after five. I waited as long as I could, but I had to be somewhere."

"I went to the USO about then—to see if you might have left a message there. I wasn't gone long."

"The USO. I didn't think about that. It's not something a girl would think of." The quick smile again. "Not being a sailor or a soldier or anything." She looked away briefly and then looked back.

"I guess not."

"So what do we do now?" she asked. "I mean, it might seem strange for me to say it after leaving you stranded for several hours, but I did make a special trip just to spend some time with you."

I don't know how long it was before I responded, "Well, I guess we can get something to eat if you're hungry."

"Starved," she said. "You?"

"Had a hot dog. But I can use some dessert."

"I'll buy you a hot fudge sundae while I have some spaghetti. It's the least I can do."

"All right," I said.

I fell in beside her, painfully aware that we had not even embraced but still unable to let myself forgive her. She wrapped both arms around my dangling right arm and leaned her head into my shoulder as we walked.

"I'm really so sorry," she said. "I did try to find you, but I was just so involved. I joined in with a group marching through downtown. They told me about a rally in Central Park at six o'clock. I thought it was really important. And it was."

"I understand," I said. And I did. The anger subsided quickly, but the warmth was not back. I did take her hand but I was not ready to do more.

The little restaurant we found did not serve ice cream, but I did enjoy the apple pie and my humpteenth cup of coffee that day. We sat across from each other at a little round table against a wall. Julie loved spaghetti and I usually kidded her about twirling it up on her fork and turning her head sideways, as she was doing now, to get it all in. 'Why don't you just cut it up in little pieces like I do?" I would say, but she never would. "Only country bumpkins from Texas do it that way," she would have answered, "not us country bumpkins from New York—state, that is."

Seeing this familiar scene before me, remembering that familiar exchange, I began to soften. "I wish you would hurry up and swallow that mouthful," I said. "I want to climb over this table and kiss you."

She didn't look up. She swallowed, then wiped her lips with her napkin. Sliding her plate across the table, she got up and moved her chair around to my side. We squeezed our chairs into the close space, leaving enough aisle for the waiters to pass. We did not kiss at first. We embraced tightly, cheek to cheek. She whispered, "Thank you for putting up with me."

When the next waiter passed, I ordered a bottle of wine. The waiter seemed reluctant. The wine I chose was cheap, but the selection was poor. I knew that he saw his table being unprofitably occupied for much too long. I sympathized, but it couldn't be helped.

"We're not going to drink all of this, are we?"

"Why not?" I asked. "There's nothing else to do in this dead town."

She smiled and accepted my silent toast. That faraway look

was back. I tried to ignore it.

"Tell me where you've been," she said.

"Oh, come on, now," I answered. "You don't want to hear some sailor telling you about his adventures on the high seas."

"Yes, I do," she responded. "I wouldn't want to hear 'some sailor' bragging about his adventures. But I do like to watch your face when you tell me about all those new places you've seen."

And so, for awhile, I did tell her a few stories. I almost forgot the hours of waiting and wondering. This was fine, but as we talked, the anticipation of the hours ahead made it even more so. I saw Julie as she was, but I also saw her as she would be when we shut ourselves away from the rest of the city and she and I were all there was in the world.

I emptied the bottle and evened out the remainder in our glasses. "Now, tell me what you've learned in school," I said.

"I'd rather tell you about today," she answered.

I cringed. For the last hour or so, 'today' had no longer existed. I'd wiped the slate clean, but the stain returned in an instant. Julie did not seem to notice.

"I met friends and relatives of people who were killed in this war today," she said. "I learned that I've got to become much more involved than I've been before."

"I think you should," I said. "If you really feel so strongly about it."

"I do. I don't think it had ever really hit home until now. I knew it was happening, but there was something unreal about it."

"You've seen demonstrations on campus. I know. You've told me about them."

"Yes, but not like this. Those were usually people who just didn't believe in what the government is doing—what it's making kids do. But this—." She held onto my hand and I could feel her intensity in her grip. "This is big. These people are not trying to just change minds. They're trying to change policy. They're trying to stop this war."

"I know," I said. "I've seen them."

"I've been invited to a candlelight rally at one of the churches." My spirit sank with each word. "The minister is going to lead us in prayers for peace and then we'll walk silently through the streets."

"I thought you were becoming an atheist."

"I don't know—maybe—I don't know. What does it matter?"

"It matters," I said, "that this is happening on this one weekend of all weekends in the year—this weekend I had looked so forward to for so long."

"But you can come with me," she protested. "I expected you to come."

"I can't come," I said. "I'm in uniform."

"You can change. We can find something for you to wear."

"I can't," I insisted. "We're under orders. No civvies. Period. Especially this weekend."

"But that's just like—"

"No it isn't. I know exactly what you're going to say. And it isn't."

"Why not."

"Because when I took an oath, I didn't give up my conscience. I wouldn't kill people I knew were innocent just because some officer told me to. But I won't disobey this order because I believe it is right."

"But you can't believe—"

"This has nothing to do with Vietnam," I said. I seldom interrupted Julie, but I couldn't seem to stop myself now. "The ship moves on Monday. We all have to be on it. We're not fighting in Vietnam—we're patrolling the Atlantic. This is not us and the V.C.—it's us and the Soviets. They've got nuclear subs out there and we track them. Sailors who get involved in political demonstrations and get tear gassed and thrown in jail miss ship's movement. They get thrown in the brig. And they should be."

God! I'd never made a speech like that. I'd never really even thought that much about it. I was trying only to expand my horizons a bit—have some meaningful experiences while I put my college act back together. But the reality of this situation put it all into perspective. I didn't know what I believed about Vietnam except that I wished for the sake of many people that it had never happened. I did know which direction my beliefs were turning. I couldn't help that. But I also knew that this war, as big as it might be, was only one of many wars this country would fight. Men and women who had voluntarily committed a certain number of years to military service *had* given up some degree of their rights to question the validity of their nation's wars. In another year I'd regain that freedom. Now it was out of the question.

Julie was staring at me. I knew what she was preparing herself to say, so I said if for her. "You go," I said. "I can meet you when it's over. I don't care how late."

"It's an all-night vigil," she answered.

"Go anyway," I said. "You have to go. And I have to insist that you go."

"I'm sorry," she said. "I didn't plan it this way."

"I know. It happened."

"And it's so—" she held out her hand in defeat.

"Important?"

"Yes, important." She shook her head. "It sounds almost trivial when I put it that way."

"I know, Julie," I said. "But this is all real in a way that I don't think I've ever known realness." I took her hand. "Bill and I had to dodge the demonstrators today. I think a lot of the college crowd who are burning draft cards and all that made up their minds the first time they realized this might have something to do with them. I don't think a lot of'em bothered to weigh any issues before they became protesters."

Julie started to raise an argument, but I continued quickly. "Those people I saw today weren't like that. It's one thing to say 'hell, no, I won't go' and let some poor kid from the barrio or the ghetto or even the poor white neighborhood take your place. It's quite another to say 'this has gotta end.'"

"You do understand," Julie said, looking deeply into my eyes.

"Yes," I answered. "I understand. I understood when I first saw you walking toward me tonight. The question is, do you understand what *I'm* saying?"

"No," she said bluntly. "I really don't."

"I didn't expect you to," I said. "Mine's a little more difficult."

"But I know that you understand," she said. "That's what matters."

"Thanks," I said. "I don't know if that's the appropriate response, but thanks for knowing it."

I left the waiter a twenty dollar bill—half a week's pay. What did I need it for? As soon as we were on the sidewalk, I embraced Julie. She drew me toward a dark recessed store front. There we embraced and kissed for too short a time. Finally I sensed her beginning to grow anxious about the time. "I'll walk you as far as I can," I said. "Until we see the candles."

"It's not close. I'm going to have to take a taxi. Let's just stay right here until one comes along."

"Usually I'd say that might take hours," I said. "With my luck, tonight one is probably bearing down on us right now."

"I'll meet your ship when it gets back to Boston."

"That's next weekend. I've got weekend duty."

"Soon then," she said. "We'll make up for this."

"Soon," I said.

Julie, I learned from Bill, threw herself into the movement as soon as she returned to her campus. Remarkable as she was, she did so while managing to make her classes. She made time for little else. The weekend after our arrival back in Boston, I traveled to see Julie on campus. My military haircut drew stares everywhere we walked, though Julie, as always, was oblivious to others' judgmental behavior. We had no more than an hour of private time before I released her to her committees. Though we corresponded, it was almost two months before I met her again, and then it was to say goodbye.

TWENTY-EIGHT

I HAD NEVER really discussed with Melinda the troubling issues that kept my mind so confused. Perhaps it was because that had been so much a part of my relationship with Julie. Perhaps it was because I was afraid to discover that we held incompatible views. A better explanation may have been that I sought escape from the world outside of Brodie in my relationship with Melinda.

When the Democratic National Convention in Chicago was finally completed, I found myself falling into something approaching despair. I'd not expected the convention to mend the nation's wounds, but I also had not been prepared for the spectacle the nation was subjected to. Mother had watched with absolute disgust, even leaving the room at times when the activity outside became too violent. What were we coming to? I still wondered.

On the last evening, I turned the TV off early, deciding to read about the final events in the morning paper. I called Melinda and asked if she minded a visit.

When I arrived, Mr. and Mrs. Proctor were glued to the television.

"I figured you'd be watching the convention," Mr. Proctor said as Melinda escorted me through the living room into the kitchen.

Both little girls were at the table, looking pretty in their night clothes and very sleepy. I sat down while Melinda poured me a glass of iced tea. Melissa came and sat on my lap, giving me a hug. Sandra, sleepily dragging an oversized teddy bear, waited to be lifted.

"Now, don't be a bother," Melinda said to them. "He can't drink his tea with both of you up there."

"Oh, that's all right," I said. I lifted Sandra up and immediately felt sympathy for Melinda and all mothers I'd seen with children hanging all over them. But I did enjoy her children. They smelled of powder. Their innocent affection and trust proved good medicine on such a night.

Melinda came and picked Sandra and her teddy bear off my lap. "It's time you two were in bed," she said. She started toward the hallway. "Say good night, Lissa, and come along."

"I think Lissa's too sleepy to walk," I said. I picked her up and followed them down the hall. After helping to put them to bed and saying good night, I left them with their mother. I returned to the kitchen to wait. After a few minutes, Melinda returned.

"You look tired," I said. "Maybe I shouldn't have come."

"No, no," she protested. "I'll have some iced tea with you and I'll be fine. Actually, I needed some company."

"I was feeling a bit restless, myself."

"The convention?"

"And other things. There's too much going on at once."

"It's not much like when we were in high school."

"Has it occurred to you," I said, "that we've never danced together?"

"The summer has gone by quickly."

"I mean, even in high school we never had dances. Is the 'Bible Belt' attitude still so strong here?"

"I think it's changing some. They have junior-senior proms at school now. The whole world is changing."

"Some things should change," I said. "Some things shouldn't." She looked at me, waiting for an explanation. I felt too tired to explain, even to decide what I'd meant by it. "Yes, the whole world is changing."

"Would you like to go outside where we can't hear the television?"

"That would be perfect," I said.

We finished our tea and left out the back door. "Sometimes I come out here after I've put the girls to bed and just take off for a walk around the neighborhood."

"Well, shall we?" I asked.

A northerly breeze was just strong enough to make the walk comfortable. We walked slowly, keeping mostly away from the more lighted streets.

It was awhile before either of us spoke, and it was Melinda who broke the silence. "You know, in spite of all those changes, good and bad, it really is good to be alive."

"Oh, I needed that," I said. "I hope you really meant it and didn't say it just to lift my spirits."

"No," she said. "I mean it."

"Well, sometimes I must be a real downer for you, but I feel the same way. I've discovered a lot of amazing and beautiful things in life the last few years."

"I'll bet you have."

I almost laughed. "I've seen a lot of strange things, too."

"When you come back from college, you're going to have a beard and long hair. And you'll be wearing a t-shirt with a peace sign painted on the front."

"Don't forget the swastika tattoo and the American flag sewed onto the seat of my pants."

"No," she said. "That's not you."

"But the rest is?"

"That's what we'll find out when you've been away to college for awhile. I don't think we know the real you yet."

I stopped and stood in front of Melinda. "You know, you're pretty smart."

"I'm a woman."

"Oh," I said, feigning shock, "the world *is* changing."

"And like you said," she responded, "some things *should* change."

We turned a corner and were headed back toward the Proctor home. I could see that the living room lights were out. "I guess I'd better get you back home," I said. "I didn't realize it was so late."

"I'd like to walk all night. But I do need to get up early."

"And you really are tired."

"Yes, but I do feel better after a walk."

The front porch light was on, so arm in arm, we walked around to the back door.

"How would you like to go dancing next Saturday?" I asked. Melinda walked silently beside me. "Well," I said, "you don't seem very enthusiastic about the prospect."

We were at the door. Melinda stood before me, her arms on my shoulders, her eyes cast down. "And when will you be going away?" she finally asked.

"Sunday morning."

She looked up. Her eyes reflected a distant light. "How about a picnic instead?"

"A picnic it is." I smiled. "Actually, I think I'd like that much better."

"And just the two of us. Don't be polite and ask about bringing the girls."

"Just the two of us, then."

We said good bye and I drove toward home, but before I got there I turned north and drove out of town, away from the main highway, away from Zack's and mother's farms, away from all of Brodie and its surroundings.

I didn't know if Melinda had sensed how much she had helped me tonight, but she had revealed to me a truth about myself that I had not clearly seen. So much was being said recently about 'finding oneself.' I had been among the scoffers. But what Melinda had said was true. I had been questioning all summer—in fact, I had been questioning for the last year or two who I really was inside. Or, maybe, everyone had the idea all wrong; maybe, it should be stated as finding who one was destined to become. What I needed was time away—away from the Navy, away from my home and its reminders of too-recent sorrows, and, yes, even time away from Melinda and the comfort of her embrace. I needed the challenge of an entirely new surrounding. That was what had driven me to a university across the state, hidden in the tall dark pines of East Texas, so very different from the open and windy plains. If I did not find myself there, I would find the path that I would follow, perhaps, for years to come.

TWENTY-NINE

I N MY THREE months at home, I had managed to disarrange my bedroom until it was almost mine again. And yet the room had felt like no more than a resting place. My worldly possessions consisted of several pairs of jeans and assorted shirts, one suit, four or five ties, two jackets, two pairs of shoes, a cheap phonograph and small record collection, a pretty good camera, a stack of paperback books, my 1954 Chevy, and a beat-up old Gretsch flat top guitar. The seabag and its contents had been stored in the attic, awaiting the end of my two-year stand-by reserve obligation. All the rest would be in the Chevy before daylight on Sunday.

"Alan." It was Mother's voice from the living room.

"Yes?"

"Could you come in here a minute? I have some things you might want to take."

"Coming."

Mother was sitting on the couch when I entered. In front of her, on the coffee table, was a cardboard box. "I want you to take this picture."

I took the framed photograph in my hand. It was a portrait of Daddy and Mother, taken soon after they were married. Daddy was in his Army uniform and Mother in a high-shouldered suit with a large pin on the lapel. As long as I could remember, it had hung in the hallway.

"I couldn't take this," I said.

"I want you to. I have another in the album. I'm planning to have it enlarged and framed."

"Thank you." I placed it inside the box.

"And this," she said, holding up a Bible, "was your Daddy's. If you open it, you'll see it says, 'To Daddy from your son Alan, Christmas 1952.' It's in your handwriting."

"I remember."

"I don't know that he ever opened it up, except the few times I managed to get him to church, but he was proud of it."

I suppressed a smile. "Maybe I'll do better with it," I said.

"And here are some other of his things—his hairbrush, his travel bag, and a few other items you might use."

"I'll take them all."

She packed everything into the box while I sat beside her. Outside, late morning sun brightened the yard. The tabletop fan moaned and clattered in the kitchen. Two sparrows argued on a rosebush.

"I hope you'll write with a little more regularity than you did in the Navy."

"I promise."

"I'll write as often as I can. Of course, there won't be much of importance happening here."

"Everything of importance to me happens here."

"Oh, I don't believe that," Mother said. "Besides, you'll find more and more matters of importance where you are."

"Maybe. But I still want to know everything that happens here. I want to know about your classes and about the crops. I want to know when they tear a building down, or even if old Edgar Lyons ever gets defeated for Mayor."

"I'll tell you all I can."

"Thanks." I closed up the box and held it in my lap, preparing to take it into the bedroom with the others. "One thing I know," I said. "I sure am going to miss your cooking."

Mother laughed. "I think you're just going to miss having your meals cooked *for* you."

"Well, that's part of it," I confessed. "But TV dinners and frozen pies just ain't gonna be the same as home cookin'."

"You'd better do better than that. You can prepare a pretty decent meal when you want to."

"The trouble with mothers," I said, "is that they take their skills for granted. It takes more than throwing a little grub in the pan to put a good dinner on the table."

"You'll manage," she said. "When you stop being a chauvinist and use your own skills."

"Manage or starve, I suppose."

"Oh," Mother said as she stood, "Zack called while you were outside cleaning the car."

"What did he have to say?"

"He just said he'd like to see you before you go."

"I was planning to drop by on the way out in the morning."

"I guess he just wanted to be sure he didn't miss you."

"I'll call him after while."

"Are you still going to have lunch with Melinda?"

"Yes. She gets off at twelve on Saturdays. We're going to ride out to Buffalo Lakes."

"I hope you have a nice drive," Mother said. I smiled. "Melinda is a nice young woman."

"I know."

The sun shone bright as we headed toward the lakes. I tried to keep my eyes off the fields we passed until we were well beyond the hail-damaged area. But I couldn't get over the abundance surrounding me, even though the drought had made it less than a bumper year. One maize crop was already being combined. Others were red carpets in the distance, almost ripe. A few white bolls speckled some of the dryland cotton crops as we neared the canyon. But the first cotton stripping would be a least a month away.

Melinda sat close to me, her warmth resting on my shoulder. We talked small talk, avoiding subjects, saving them for the lakeside.

Five miles before the lakes, the terrain began to change. On one side of the highway were sloping fields; on the other, bushy mesquites and pasture land. Two miles more and we were completely out of the farm land and into ranch country. We could have been a hundred miles from Brodie. But if we had continued across the canyon another two miles, we would have been back above the caprock and among other flatland fields of cotton and maize.

Outside the gate, at a roadside stand, we stopped for cold cider before continuing on into the park. A few minutes later, we were out of the car, sitting on the grass overlooking a draw and shaded by giant old cottonwoods. The lake water was a pretty blue, nothing like the ocean, calm except for the rolling vee's of water trailing pleasure boats and skiers. Shouts from swimmers and skiers, laughter from picnickers, outboard motor noise, transistor radios, bird songs, splashing of fish in the draw—all made for pleasant chatter. Out in the water, in the smaller of the lakes, open boats of serious catfishermen rested, still and patient, their drab-clothed occupants immobile. On the other lake, speedboats whirred and growled, zigzagging from the bridge to the dam and dangerously near the shore. Skiers in minimal bathing suits and bright orange life jackets danced over the surface, leaning into turns, occasionally disappearing with violent splashes.

"It's a pretty day," Melinda said.

"Yes, it is."

She took my hand. "You're not saying much today. I mean, you always have been quiet, but you don't have much at all to say today."

"I'm sorry." I met her gaze and then looked away.

"I don't envy you," she said. "It's never easy to go through a transition. At least it never has been for me."

"Nor for anyone, I suppose," I answered. "I've left for college before. I've joined the Navy. I've come home. Maybe it's the fear we get that things won't turn out as well as we'd hoped." I faced Melinda again. "Do you want to know what was really on my mind just now?"

"Yes, if you want me to know."

"I do. I was wondering how different it would be if I weren't going back to school, if I'd come home to stay. I was wondering how different things might have been for us."

It was Melinda's time to turn away. "Oh? And would your feelings have been different?"

"Maybe in some ways. My feelings would have been more free to grow."

Melinda remained silent, her face expressionless. The lake and trees moved about her in profile. Leaf shadows made playful patterns on her skin. After a long moment, she turned to me and smiled. "It's been a nice summer, hasn't it?"

"It has."

"You've made it a nice summer for me. I want you to know that."

"I'm glad."

"Maybe," she said, "things might have gone a little slower if we hadn't tried to pack too much into a few months." She looked back toward the lake. "If I hadn't known that you'd only be home for that little time, I might not have allowed myself to feel anything at all."

"I never wanted to rush you," I said.

She turned back to me and took my hand. "And you never did. That's one thing that made it so nice."

I looked at Melinda and wondered. I realized that there were many important things I didn't know about her, nor she about me. I knew only that I enjoyed being with her, that she was good, that I almost desired her now, that she needed time away from stress—away even from me.

For an hour, we sat on the grass, sipping our soft cider, remembering the summer. When the sun broke between the trees, we got up and walked down a foot trail past the picnic tables with their carved and painted messages—Brad loves Susan, Seniors '65—, behind boat stalls, and finally onto a deserted, rotting fishing pier. We walked out to the edge and stood watching, taking in the breeze, the coolness of the lake.

We stood without speaking for awhile, arm in arm, knowing that this might be the last time.

"Where do we go from here?" I asked.

"I don't know. I guess we just go on living for now."

I took a deep breath. Melinda's thoughts, I knew, were not of the present. I pondered why I, in times of parting with someone I cared for, always thought of something else, even though I'd try to concentrate on the moment.

"What are your plans now?" I asked.

"When I save a little money, I'll move out of Brodie and try to make a home for my girls. We may move to Dallas. I think it's time we found a place to ourselves."

"Dallas is a three-hour drive from Huntsville. I could come up and see you occasionally."

"My plans aren't definite," she answered. "But I think I'd like that." She unwrapped her arm from mine and walked to the very end of the pier, sitting on the rough, weathered planks, with her legs dangling over the water. I sat beside her, folding my arms in front of me. "What you may not understand," Melinda said, "is how very hurt I was—and still am. A divorce may not be the worst thing a person can go through, but I wouldn't want to go through anything worse. Or go through the same thing again, for that matter."

"No, I didn't understand," I said simply.

"Melissa keeps asking about her Daddy. She didn't at first. Sandra doesn't really understand what has happened, but now they're both beginning to wonder and to ask questions." I could see in Melinda's eyes the struggle against the pain. I put my arm around her again. "I can't explain to them why we'll never all be together again."

"I suppose the hurt you've gone through is different from anything I've known. I lost two people who were very close to me, but we loved each other until the moment of death. But they've left me with good memories. It's the memories that I love now."

Melinda leaned against me. "I'm glad you came back when you did," she said. "You've given me good memories. You let me use you just to have some good memories."

"Use me anytime. I can use some more good memories."

She brought herself very near, looking deeply into my eyes. "I'm so glad you were here," she said. "I'm a crazy, mixed-up lady, but you've brought me back to life."

I kissed her and smiled. "I like crazy, mixed-up ladies," I said. And then I kissed her again.

THIRTY

SAYING GOODBYE to Mother was not easy, but she did the best for me that she could. An odd assortment of emotions pulled at me from every direction, ruining Mother's special breakfast for me, spoiling the excitement I'd wanted to feel. But Mother was grand. Nothing in her manner indicated anything but joy for my adventure and profound confidence in me. I only hoped that I would not betray that confidence.

My sleep had been interrupted once more by thunder and bursts of lightning. According to the early weather report, heavy thundershowers were an almost certainty by mid-morning. Maybe they had delayed too long. But maybe not. I wanted to stay and see the rain. But more than that, I wanted to be gone. My whole summer had been geared for this day of departure; my car was packed and ready; an unseen apartment waited for me five hundred miles away. Only goodbyes remained here.

Today I would again leave the Caprock, this high, familiar ground. I would traverse a canyon, perhaps finally receiving the nourishment it craved from above. But it would be a dark canyon under the current clouds. The abandoned highways would still invite, but less so today. Years without proper maintenance and faded warning signs could make their slippery paths treacherous if the rains I feared but longed for did arrive. I would stick to the familiar for now. I owed it to those I loved to have a safe journey until I'd arrived at my destination.

In this drugged, predawn hour, I shared one last cup of coffee with Mother, my traveling clothes on, my thermos the only thing left to carry out. Over the sink, the window was still black.

Mother's perfect kitchen surrounded me, telling me that no matter what lay ahead, *this* would always be my definition of *home*.

"I hope you keep ahead of the rain today," Mother said. "The front will be traveling your way."

"I've always liked driving in the rain."

"Even so, I'm a mother, and mothers don't like to know that their sons are out in bad weather."

"I'm glad you didn't see my ship during the hurricane."

"So am I."

The living room windows rattled with a boom of thunder. Leaves blown by a wet gust fluttered into view over the sink, the leaves momentarily green from the kitchen light. I expected raindrops at any second.

"I know I'm forgetting something," I said. "I always feel that way when I'm about to leave a place."

"I'll mail it to you if I find anything."

To put off the leaving for one more moment, I searched for something to say. Mother's eyes told me there *was* nothing more. The time had come. I got up and took my cup to the sink. Mother lingered at the table, and then she, too, brought her cup over.

"I guess this is it," I said. "Walk with me to the door."

I took my thermos from the table and put my other arm around Mother as we walked. The living room was dark, but the porch light was on. Outside, my Chevy was parked in the drive, its grille facing the street. Stopping at the open door, I turned to Mother and embraced her.

"Don't forget to go by Zack's."

"I won't. He's probably up and waiting for me."

"It's been so good to have you home."

My chest tightened, but I took control. "I'll be back before you know it."

"Please call me when you get to Huntsville."

"That's the first thing I'll do."

"Good." She patted me on the back, and we exchanged kisses. "Now you run along. It'll be raining soon."

She held the screen open and I stepped onto the porch, holding onto her hand until the last moment. "I love you, Mother."

"I love you, too."

"Goodbye."

"Goodbye. Drive safely."

I let go her hand and walked quickly to the car, not looking back until I was inside. The old engine caught with the twist of the starter and sputtered only a few seconds before settling into a comfortable purr. I shifted into first, then waved to Mother at the door and released the clutch.

Driving down the street and turning onto Main, I held my handkerchief in my lap, just in case. But I felt no sadness nor even emptiness. I felt only the supreme unimportance of the hour, the feeling of being no longer a part of my past, not yet into my future.

Orderly storefronts filed past my windows for final inspection. Shades of gray. Railroad tracks rumbled underneath my tires. I turned at the last intersection before the highway and its blinking red light.

This town needed time. It needed the war to end before it came to grips with its loss, and, God! I hoped it would have no more losses. I would find it changed each time I returned, but change would come slowly and, in some ways, would be perceptible only to those who truly loved it.

Five minutes later I left the pavement for a dirt country road. First light of morning faintly reflected in my rearview mirror. As yet—no raindrops.

Leaving the county road, I headed up the turn row to Zack's. Soft dirt spun the tires in a rut filled with topsoil, and then the surface became hard and bumpy. Off to one side, illuminated by my bouncing headlights, stood barren patches of cotton stalks, trying to make a comeback after the hail. Ahead was Zack's house and the light at the kitchen window.

I made the curve around the toolshed and parked behind Zack's pickup. Zack was at the screen door.

"Good morning," I called.

"Morning'. Come inside before it gets wet."

"Think it will?"

"Don't see why not." He followed me into the kitchen. "Saw you comin' up the road. Your coffee's poured."

Spider stood up and shook his bones, his tail waving at half mast. I reached for his head and he licked my hand. His mournful old eyes looked into mine.

"Mornin', old boy," I said to him, scratching behind his ears. A front paw came up to my shin and settled by my foot.

"Are you packed and ready?" Zack asked.

"I'm on my way."

We took our coffee cups to the table. Zack sipped slowly from his. I was on my third cup of the day, but then, it was a coffee kind of morning.

"I wish you could stay to see the rain."

"So do I."

Zack drummed his fingers uncharacteristically on the table. "I know you're gonna have to hit the pavement pretty quick before it gets wet out," he said, "but I'm glad you came by."

As if on cue, a bolt of lightning to the south brightened the yard and shook the house. Spider crawled up against my chair. Zack looked outside.

"Maybe I *had* better be going," I said. Reluctantly, I drained my cup, patted Spider's raised head, and prepared to go.

Zack followed me outside. "I don't know if I'd've made it this summer without your help," he said.

"Sure you would've. Besides, I enjoyed every minute of it." I grinned. "Well, almost every minute."

"Just the same, I appreciated it."

We went over to my car. I stood by the front bumper, and Zack leaned back on the tailgate of his pickup. Looking away, he searched the clouds, now red and orange to the west, with gray fringes overhead. "You know," he began, hesitating, "I had me a son once that I thought about makin' into a farmer." He pulled out a cigar and bit off the end. "But—." He spat. "He didn't take to it. His momma already had him made into a city boy—a Californian. He's got another Daddy now, a lot younger than his first one. Three years ago last May, I let him be adopted. Figured that was right."

I didn't know what was coming, but I was uncomfortable listening. I, too, looked away. "I remember your boy," I said. "I didn't get the impression he was very excited about this part of the country."

Zack slowly chewed his cigar. "No, he just didn't take to it."

I knew that this must be painful to Zack, but I sensed that he wanted to talk about it. "Do you see him still?"

"Not since he was adopted. We send Christmas cards. That's about all."

"I didn't know."

Zack shifted his weight. "Well, I reckon that's how it oughta be. He's still got my blood runnin' in him, but he had a right to pick who his daddy was. He was old enough for that." He paused again, turning to spit a piece of tobacco into the pickup bed. "Anyway, I'm up past sixty now. Be hittin' seventy in a few years. Figure I've got some farmin' to do yet, but you never know when your time will come."

I interrupted. "You've got a lot of farming to do," I said, feeling at the same time, and for the first time, that Zack was becoming an old man.

"Maybe," he acknowledged. "But even so, I figured I'd better go have a talk with Mr. Riley. Had it wrote up so's my boy can get anything that the cows bring and what's left when my equipment's auctioned. Got a bit of money set aside, too."

My breath stopped. I looked hard into Zack's eyes. But he was still looking away.

"I'd always meant that you and David should have the farm."

Pain gripped my chest. "Zack—"

"It'll be yours now—when I'm gone."

I wanted to run. "You can't do that."

"It's done." He looked imploringly into my eyes. "It wouldn't mean anything to my boy."

"But I can't say I'll ever farm it."

"Didn't expect you to. Leastwise not now. You see, there's one thing about ownin' a farm. When times get hard, you can always come back to it, and even if you can't scratch out a livin,' you got a place to be."

I pulled out my handkerchief. No argument I could think of could counter Zack's determination. If I had been in his shoes, I would have done the same thing, and he and I both knew it. Carefully, I folded the handkerchief and returned it to my back pocket. "I don't know what to say."

"Ain't nothin' *to* say. I'm layin' a big burden on you. You probably oughta kick my butt." He put his cigar away and pushed himself off the tailgate. "Now you better get on down the road before it's too late."

I laughed. "Zack, you're a rich man."

"Shoot!" He turned to look at his ancient pickup, his bleak, stuccoed house, his damaged crops out in the darkness. "You got 'bout enough brains to be a farmer."

I took his hand. "This is gonna take some thinking."

"Save your thinkin' for college," Zack said. "Now, get on outa here."

The rain hit before I'd traveled half a mile on the main highway. I was alone. No headlights came toward me. Another mile and the sky broke loose. The countryside, only beginning to be visible, suddenly disappeared. With any luck, the downpour would settle into the gentle, lingering rain the crops had so long thirsted for. With any luck, it might still do some good. But the rain became even heavier. I turned the windshield wipers to 'high.' Swish. Swish. Swish. I could hardly see the highway ahead.

End

www.ingramcontent.com/pod-product-compliance
Lightning Source LLC
Chambersburg PA
CBHW060935180626
46817CB00004B/1564